PROLESCARYET

TALES OF HORROR AND CLASS WARFARE

EDITED BY

Ian Bain, Anthony Engebretson, J.R. Handfield,
Eric Raglin, and Marcus Woodman

Cover art copyright © 2021 by Lynne Hansen, LynneHansenArt.com

Editors: Ian Bain, Anthony Engebretson, J.R. Handfield, Eric Raglin, and Marcus Woodman

Interior Design, Typesetting, and Layout: Sam Richard

CONTENTS

INTRODUCTION

We've all had those weeks.

You know the ones we're talking about. You got written up because you didn't meet the arbitrary numbers cooked up by an algorithm, you were forced to stay late to fix someone else's problem, your landlord wouldn't deal with the family of mice that took up residence in your wall, the customer that always harasses you came in again and you would have told him to shove it if you didn't need that job to pay (most of) your bills...

No matter where you are, no matter what you do, you're running in place—if not falling behind—while your boss cruises in an hour late, parks his Tesla across two parking spaces, and barks orders at you between sips of an over-priced chain latte.

And it makes you *angry*.

You're angry because you're not in this spot due to any choices *you* made. You're angry because so many other people are in the same spot. Because it feels like the bad guys are winning again.

If you've picked this book up, chances are you've felt that

way before or feel that way now. You recognize that the problems you deal with, the debts you owe, and the long hours at the desk are systemic and pervasive and all-consuming. You've picked this book up because you enjoy the horror genre, but you also recognize that life under capitalism is a horror story in and of itself.

The horrors of capitalism are the horrors we all face every day. We confront them head-on through the lens of horror, dark, and speculative fiction within the pages of *ProleSCARYet: Tales of Horror and Class Warfare*. This anthology includes nineteen tales of capitalism gone wrong —from designer children to deadly bosses, predatory lenders to plague-ridden laborers. Each story provides a perspective on the dark underbelly of economic oppression through some of horror's best independent and emerging writers from around the globe.

ProleSCARYet is a fully independent effort organized by five individuals from across North America collaborating remotely during the COVID-19 crisis. The editors compensated each featured writer for their work and did not charge a submission fee—practices they'd like to see become the norm in publishing. Profits from this collection will be directed to Labor Rights, an organization in solidarity with workers around the world fighting for better pay, better work conditions, and a better quality of life.

The horror genre allows us to turn our gaze to the disgusting, the profane, and the unacceptable that exists within our society. We hope these stories provide solace, guidance, and support, no matter your status or situation. And remember: "What the bourgeoisie therefore produces, above all, are its own grave diggers. Its fall and the victory of the proletariat are equally inevitable." —Karl Marx

VARIABLES

CLARK BOYD

The poisonous air of the Gulf Coast damages everything it touches.

My late mother's beater, a wheezing Saturn with 150,000 miles and jagged rust spots poking through the powder blue paint, is a testament to that. As is the person approaching that car, balancing a dozen tepid pizzas and fumbling for the keys.

It wasn't an integral part of my Life Plan to end up as a middle-aged "pizza transportation professional" in the sweat-slicked folds of America's armpit. I wish I could say that it was the plague and the plague alone that put me in this position, but it's probably more complicated than that. The sickness—its relentless death march and humanity's blindness to it—certainly didn't help. First, it took away my already tenuous livelihood as an adjunct math teacher at the local community college, leaving me with few alternatives other than driving greasy, mediocre pies around the panhandle.

Then it took the only person who ever really cared about me—my mother.

She died a few weeks ago. Alone. I wasn't allowed to visit her in the hospital and only found out later that she never received last rites. The current plague rules forced me to have her cremated; she was deathly afraid of fire. Her funeral service was a pathetic affair with only myself and a Catholic deacon, both masked and distant, in attendance. The parish, I was told, was so busy with other funerals that a real priest wasn't available. Only for the powerful and wealthy, I suppose, and my mother was neither.

She loved gardening, and would often tell me she dreamed of lying in eternal peace beneath a well-manicured gravesite with plenty of colorful flowers. Instead, she's currently riding shotgun in a makeshift urn made of gray plastic.

I've been waiting for the appropriate time and place to say my final goodbye to her. She deserves to be treated well in death, because she did an amazing job of raising me, by herself, in life. Between daily shifts at the diner and Wal-Mart, she not only kept me fed and clothed but also found time to support my academic pursuits.

When I was younger, I loved algebra and its relentless push to solve for X. A shy and socially invisible girl, I sometimes fantasized that *I* was X, the variable, the object of everyone's fascination, however short-lived it was. I reveled in those math classes, pencil sharpened and head bent low, trying to balance increasingly complex equations.

Adding and multiplying. Reluctantly dividing. Subtracting as a last resort.

My classmates only seemed interested in getting the right answer, in finishing the assignment with the absolute minimum amount of effort and understanding. That is, after all, what most of our teachers rewarded. But I lived for the process, for discovering meaning within the mechanics. All those ways to potentially reach an answer? To me, that wasn't confusing or disheartening. It was a glimpse into a world full of potential. Liberating.

There were times I'd work out a complicated problem over the course of an hour, marvel at the beauty of the path I took, and then entirely forget to note my solution. But I always made sure to show my work, to provide proof that I saw the bigger picture. To make it clear to my teachers that I *understood* precisely what was at stake in every mathematical puzzle. In return, I was often penalized.

"I need solutions, Lindy," said Mr. Marvin, who held dominion over my 11th grade Algebra 2 class. "When you grow up, you'll find that employers need answers, not elegance."

Maybe if I had approached things differently back then, I wouldn't be putting a dozen tainted pizzas on the car seat next to my mother's ashes right now. Then again, there's a chance I was always headed in this direction. Before I turn the key and begin my delivery run, my mind snags on a related question that's haunted me lately: is it better to wrap yourself in willful ignorance and believe you're right no matter what, or to wage a worthy, yet losing battle with the deeper truths that lie buried in the rancid muck of ambiguity? Mathematical or otherwise, I mean.

Shit, I don't know. I just deliver pizzas. The only constant in my life now is that no matter how much deodorizer I use, I can't rid Mom's car of the reek of onions, spicy processed meats, and half-burnt mozzarella.

I put the Saturn into drive.

This will be the very definition of a special delivery.

———

LOCHLEVEN IS A "COVENANT-CONTROLLED COMMUNITY" not far from the beach.

Just before the turn-in is a billboard featuring a beaming family of four. All white, of course. Dad holds a golf club, while Mom clutches a Bible. Covenant-controlled, indeed. The kids look as if they're ready for a day at the beach. Or maybe it's soccer practice. The older one might be about ready to nail her SATs and go to Princeton. Underneath this tableau, in red, white, and blue letters, is the elevator pitch: "American Paradise… at the Right Price."

Paradise is guarded by Cliff, who is asleep when I pull up. His faux tartan mask is pulled down below his nose, and the cloth moves in and out with each shallow breath. I tap on the window of his booth to wake him. Startled, he reaches for his gun and begins waving it at me. There's no need to panic. Cliff's gun is real, but the homeowners' association won't let him put bullets in it. He let that secret slip once in between sour sips of the bourbon he puts in his coffee mug while he's on duty.

Cliff pulls down his mask and barks at me through his brain fog.

"What the hell do you want?"

"It's me, Mr. Dyer. Pizza delivery. Same as always."

He looks my car up and down and grimaces. Eventually, he nods and puts the gun away. Then he pushes the button to raise the gate and waves me through. In the rearview, I watch as he props his feet back up on the guard desk and leans his head back.

As I drive on, I glance at the order slip again. A dozen pies for "Plague Party." That's the name they gave when they placed the order.

"Pretty funny, huh?" I ask Mom.

She doesn't seem inclined to answer.

My destination, 2247 Liberty Lane, can only be described as a McMansion. For a lover of numbers like myself, this place is an odd sort of heaven. On the way over, I looked up the address on one of those real estate apps on my phone. The home itself is 7,000 square feet. There are six bedrooms and five full baths spread out over three floors and a full basement. It's also got a 50-yard pool with four lanes, and a game room. All on ten acres of land. Its "signature features" are two turrets that rise high above the third floor.

Call it Swamp Tudor with a touch—a soupçon if you will —of Late Medieval.

As I slowly make my way around the circular drive, I notice two giant floodlights throwing shadows on the façade. "Façade" is an apt description of the whole thing, inside and out. The company that built this house, and hundreds like it around here, is continually being sued for shoddy workmanship, not to mention dozens of code violations. The owner likes to cut corners. If you slam an upstairs door in one of his houses, the basement walls will shake.

Worst of all, the builder disregards all of the city's plague regulations. Since the beginning of the sickness a few years ago, company officials have repeatedly failed to enforce distancing and mask rules for their construction workers, some of whom have gotten sick and died as a result. Management gets away with minor fines because the owner is drinking buddies with the mayor. And gives generously to his reelection campaigns.

But hey, who cares about a little corruption, right? Turrets! A touch of classy Olde England right here in the panhandle. The perfect spot, judging by more than one of the houses in Lochleven, from which to proudly fly your Confederate flag.

I park at the bottom of the marble steps that lead up to the entry, which is framed by two Ionic columns. The door is meant to look like oak, but I can tell it's fake wood. Almost every light in the house is on. All of the windows are wide open too, even though I can hear the air conditioner running. The dull thump of electronic bass overlaid with the trebly squeals and cackles of unsuspecting youth trickles out into the night.

Under the plague rules, gatherings of more than ten people are not allowed.

But those rules, as anyone in this house would tell you, don't apply in Lochleven.

A young woman stands at one of the turret windows, her form illuminated by the big halogen lamps in the garden below. The thrown shadows of a weeping willow, moving in the Gulf breeze, sway around her. For a moment, I can't shake the notion that they're skeletal fingers, reaching and clawing their way toward her. She wears nothing but panties and a bra. The cigarette I see burning brightly between her lips means one thing to me. She's not wearing a mask. Another rule broken. I want to wave at her, to warn her about any number of approaching dangers. But just as I open my mouth, a thick arm appears from the shadows behind her. It circles her waist and, with a sudden jerk, pulls her back into the darkness of the room. The turret echoes with a shriek followed by laughter. I'm too late, it seems.

I circle the car to get the pizzas.

Before I pick them up, though, I gently pat the top of Mom's urn. Then I reach into my back pocket and grab my mask. I'm a stickler for the rules of what people call, even after five years of rampant death, "the new normal." I use the car's passenger-side mirror to ensure the cloth covers my nose and mouth. This beauty, which I sewed myself, is deep red. Maybe I was inspired by pizza sauce. Or by something more sinister. Across the front of the mask, I've stitched a skeleton's mouth frozen in a rictus grin. When it's positioned right, it looks as if all the flesh from the lower half of my jaw has been stripped away.

I pause to admire my handiwork.

The mirror reminds me that I'm closer than I appear.
Like Death.

———

I'M A BIT OLD-FASHIONED, I guess, when it comes to mass
murder.

Arsenic was once called "inheritance powder." Back in the
day, when forensics wasn't as advanced as it is now, young
dukes and marquises used it as an almost foolproof way to
kill their daddies and uncles. You know, get a jump start on
all that wealth and all those titles. The chemical was almost
impossible to detect, and many physicians thought people
poisoned by it were just dying of cholera. Over the years,
though, arsenic fell out of favor. Advances in detection
forced would-be murderers to stop using it, and that, in turn,
meant that the police stopped looking for it.

That's good news for me. Thanks to my mother, the
gardener, I have a shed full of arsenic-based insecticides.

As a murder weapon, arsenic ticks all my boxes. It's color-
less, odorless, and tasteless. That means these Plague Party
assholes, who continue to uncaringly spread the disease to
vulnerable people like my mother, won't be able to tell their
Meat Supremes have been blighted. Also, the long time
between the onset of symptoms and death ensures their
suffering will be protracted. Finally, the violent diarrhea and
endless vomiting associated with arsenic poisoning mimic
the symptoms of this cursed virus' latest strain. In the throes
of intense gastric discomfort, I sincerely hope my victims
will sit on their toilets wondering if a dump truck full of
cosmic karma hasn't just run over their smug superiority.

Twice. Hell, three times just for good measure.

That thought has me smiling as I reach for the decorative
brass knocker attached to the door. It's a badly sculpted

horse's head. For a moment, I imagine it's the trusty steed of one of the Four Horsemen of the Apocalypse. Pestilence. Yes, that would make it an entirely appropriate way for Death to announce herself.

Knock, knock.

Eventually, a young man clad only in swim trunks answers the door, beer in hand.

"Sick mask, dude," he says.

"Dudette," I shoot back.

"Ah, yeah. Couldn't tell. Sorry, bro."

He hands me a $100 bill.

"Can you put them in different rooms? Leave them wherever."

"Sure," I say. "By the way, you didn't take advantage of your free topping."

His mouth hangs open, and he snorts. I've clearly just blown his mind.

"There's a special 'Plague Party' special right now," I explain, warming quickly to the lie. "You order a two-topping pizza, and get a third topping for free. We call it our 'End of the World' deal." More stunned silence. The universe even provides him with free pizza toppings during trying times. "So, I added something to your order. I hope you enjoy it."

He hands me another bill, a 20 this time, and walks toward the back of the house, presumably to share news of this amazing good fortune with his fellow revelers.

I get to work, moving quickly through the rooms, leaving poisoned pizzas in my wake. One on the dining room table, one on the pool table in the game room, one at the end of the diving board. To great applause, I interrupt a naked co-ed sauna session with a large sausage and onion.

"Skeletor! You're our hero!" squeals one of the girls.

There are so many rooms in the house that I'm out of

pizzas before I can make it up to the turrets. Maybe that girl I saw earlier will escape death after all. But I doubt it.

I make my way back downstairs. Then I stand at the door and survey my work. Before me, I see the stoned and sloshed, the guilty and damned, eating slice after arsenic-laced slice and screaming song lyrics into each other's faces.

I wait for a hiccup of remorse, but it never comes.

I get in my car and put the Plague Party in my rearview, taking time to check out my mask again. Although I'm technically out of harm's way, I decide to leave it on.

———

EVEN THE GRIM REAPER appreciates a seaside view after a hard day at work.

I know a place that overlooks the Gulf not far from Lochleven. I remember riding out here with Mom, back in the days that now richly deserve to have "good old" attached to them, thanks to the plague. On Sunday evenings, we'd grab some ice cream, park in the dunes, and watch the buoys wink red and green across the water. Left and right, she taught me, port and starboard. Guideposts for finding your way to safe harbor.

I breeze past Cliff, who takes a long pull from his mug after seeing my mask. Then I point the rusty Saturn toward the ocean and roll down the window. Ten minutes later, I cut the engine, but leave the parking lights on. The moon is rising over the dunes.

"Mom, we're here," I say.

In the silence that follows, I puzzle over an equation that still doesn't feel balanced.

I have two variables left to deal with. The first is my mother's ashes. That one seems easy now. She loved this place as much as any. So, I once again get out of the car and walk around to the passenger side. I grab the urn, remove the top, and throw what's left of my mother up into the warm and swirling wind. Through the car lights, I watch her ashes drift out over the sand. Beneath my mask, I mumble three furtive Hail Marys.

Then I whisper, "I'm sorry." But for what exactly, I really couldn't say.

It's now time to wrestle with the final, most nagging variable of all.

I go to the trunk and retrieve a long piece of garden hose that Mom kept there for some reason. I stick one end in the tailpipe and drag the other through the open window as I get back in the car. I roll the window up as tightly as I can. In the enclosed space, the dirty sweat sock reek of old cheese seeps through the mask and gags me.

I've been working on this part of the equation, this last variable, for 50-odd years. I've tried everything I can think of to balance it more elegantly. Continuing education classes, applying for better jobs, even makeovers and hot yoga. I tried a husband for a few years—a disaster. Always adding, never subtracting. Life already felt too empty. That's why I've been reluctant to consider solutions that required taking more away from it.

I sit for a minute and watch the lights on the water. Red, green. Left, right. Stop, go.

I take off my mask and turn it upside down. The smile is now a disjointed, horror-movie frown. Then I take a hard look at the business end of that hose. My hand slowly moves toward the car key, which is still in the ignition. Do I have the courage to turn it, though? To make the ultimate subtraction?

I'm about to crank the engine when my phone suddenly rings. My pizza-jockey conditioning kicks in and I reach for the skirling device without thinking.

I pull down the mask and croak out a tiny, but relieved, "Hello."

My employer, Prospero's Pizza, is on the line wondering where the hell I am. There are, I'm reliably and profanely informed by none other than Prospero himself, more goddamn pies to be delivered. And very few people who are willing to deliver them.

"Deliveries are all I've got right now, goddammit," he yells.

I know what's coming, so I play along. Most likely in a futile attempt to delay my reckoning with that dirty garden hose and this car's ancient engine.

"Is that because the goddamn government won't let anyone sit inside your goddamn restaurant, Mr. Prospero? Because of that fake goddamn virus created in goddamn Mongolia or Angola, or wherever?"

"You know it is. They're killing us little guys. Friggin' socialists."

Little guy? The grift is strong in this one.

I know for a fact that Prospero has 20 restaurants in this part of Florida. And that he got an infusion of cash from Uncle Sam a couple of months ago as part of a stimulus package meant for small business owners. Oh, and I know that he owns a house in Lochleven.

"I'll be right there, Mr. Prospero. Just wrapping up."

I hang up before he takes any more swings at me. Or the "socialists."

It strikes me that my work on this planet may not be quite finished after all. That there will be more Plague Parties filled with more pieces of excrement who have, in all likelihood, earned a visit from Death herself. And if Prospero starts to take the heat for dishing up poisoned pies to the fine sons and daughters of the panhandle, all the better.

It's safe to say I've finally made a decent case for subtraction.

Not only that, but for the first time in my life, I have no real interest in how I got there. Only the answer matters, grim though it may be.

QED.

I shove the hose out of the window, start the car, and drive inland.

THAT YE SHALL TRANSGRESS
HAILEY PIPER

You don't have the money to travel with your friends.
That's always the start of it. No money for the movies,
for the fair, for anything. They're always leaving you behind,
but this trip crosses the line. You've never been left behind so
definitively and at this distance and for too many weeks.
Snub all the sour grapes you like, but backpacking through
Europe? That's a once-in-a-lifetime experience.

Except subtract to zero in your lifetime. You've missed
out. What else is new?

Well, this streaming channel for starters. WizTravel
Virtual Tours, they call it. Put on your headphones, click the
link, skip the ads, and let my vocal descriptions carry you to
faraway lands you could never afford in the world outside.

Pathetic, you think? Maybe, but so is your bank account.
You can watch that mold spot grow in the ceiling corner of
your bedroom in this cheap apartment, Roommate Number
1 whispering alone through one wall, Roommate Number 2
moaning and very not alone through the other.

Or you can get away. For free.

That's right, listen to my soothing voice; it's how I got this job. Where to? Safari adventure on the Serengeti? Climb Mt. Everest? See every ancient Greek ruin without hopping on a single dirty tour bus? The sound is immersive, almost as if the channel's creator has recorded street ambience on location. It's like you're there.

Except you're not. There's always that layer of your brain that's only partly submerged in its globetrotting bathtub, and the rest of your exposed, wrinkly hide knows better. Faker. Wannabe. Working class, penniless hanger-on. Your friends spend the night in a hostel somewhere in the western European Union, and their stay won't turn out like those mid-2000s torture porn movies. No, they're having the time of their lives. Eating new foods, seeing exquisite sites, meeting interesting people, and probably sleeping with some of them.

In a way, they're pathetic too, aren't they? The only danger they'll find is hiking some lonely mountain pass. Maybe Shana will twist her ankle, or Terry might get food poisoning from stuffing the wrong berries in their pack, but overall, everyone will be fine.

You don't want to be fine. You're the kind who craves a genuine experience.

WizTravel offers that, too, but you can't genuinely be penniless. Our premium channel, according to comments, is like nothing else the Internet has to offer. A few call it realer than real.

Come on, it's only a few bucks. So you'll have to stretch the ramen an extra couple of days. When your friends come home, don't you wish you'll have had an experience worth telling about? I'll guide you there, a soothing voice through each video.

Sure, you're skeptical. That only makes sense—I mean,

how good can I be? Only one way to know. That's it, type in the payment info.

You're in.

The premium page highly recommends you check the introduction video, but you don't have time for that. There's no way you can afford the premium fee a second month in a row. You don't have time to waste on introductions, disclaimers, or text blobs marked "Very Important, Please Read." Crank up the volume, click a video, any video. Hurry, you don't want to be a nothing all your life, like they all knew you'd turn out.

You're descending into the bowels of an ancient Egyptian tomb. Dust crumbles from the ceiling, and hieroglyphs coat every wall. You're following a sunburned older man in white shirt and khaki shorts, some professorial type, while several younger men in similar clothes bring up the rear. They speak with English accents. Someone mentions curses and mummies, and you get the feeling you might have slipped a century in the wrong direction.

Whispers tickle the back of your head. You think it's Roommate Number 1, but there's no way a voice could puncture both your walls and headphones at this volume. No, these whispers slide between ancient surfaces and reach the underside of your mind. The language isn't yours, but spiritual fingers need no translation. They etch feeling into your skull.

Let us sleep, they tell you.

You try to warn the professor, tugging at his sleeve, but by God, you're a fool. "Find of the century!" he shouts, and then he hurries deeper into the dark, as if he's afraid you'll convince him unless he leaves you behind, same as your friends. He might even hear the whispers himself. The rumors are true—there are curses here. The guilt of discovering this place, of the sins committed by new interlopers who will follow in your footsteps, cannot be cut from your heart.

Neither can the dead. You will be old and have forgotten this place, but they won't have forgotten you. They'll be coming. Not to hurt your body, not to kill you. Why waste effort tearing into your world of life when they can wait for you in their world of the dead? Death is always a matter of time.

You click away from the video. The irritating yet familiar whispers and moans of your roommates reverberate through the walls. You're home again. But then, you were always home, weren't you? The video link reads "Ancient Egypt Adventure, 1920," but you weren't there or then. You were here and now.

Beneath the video, red text warns that not every journey is so easily escaped.

The content creator can't be serious. Or creators? You think a few 14-year-olds with excellent microphones and clever video editing skills might be the culprits. Kids do amazing things these days. They probably make more money in a month than you make in a year.

You scroll away from "Ancient Egypt Adventure, 1920," finding it isn't your taste. A little outdated, even racist to treat an ancient culture's death customs as spooky monsters. And while another video of a different excavation tempts you—the year 3152, when archeologists will puzzle over why you put your dead in boxes underground rather than feeding them to sky squids like normal people—you've had enough grave digging.

Keep scrolling. I have a special journey in mind for you.

Near the bottom of a few dozen tantalizing titles, you find a playlist marked Experienced. There's only one video, with promises of more to come. It's labeled, "The Doorways."

You signed up for a genuine experience, didn't you? Go ahead, click. Your friends won't find better in Germany or Norway. Their most dangerous doorway leads to an outhouse instead of an indoor bathroom.

Really, you're in no danger either, right? It's just the Internet. You're still home. Only your imagination takes you far away. No real threats except a malware pop-up or an invite to the wrong part of town, but you're not going anywhere. What's the worst that could happen?

You click "The Doorways."

The world blackens; the floor turns to cool granite. No halls surround you, no structure you can understand but the empty space that stretches on and on. Few details for me to describe, but follow my voice and I'll lead you to landmarks. First, focus on the russet door that stands ahead. Darkness lines its edges.

A wooden plaque reads in bold letters: That Ye Shall Transgress.

There is nothing else to do here. You can click back and try another video—no, you want to try the door? By all means then, keep watching. This isn't some interactive game, after all, and the choices here aren't yours. You can only stay or leave.

You twist the knob and enter a long, dark corridor. Every step echoes on the granite floor, heralding your arrival, and yet the sounds halt where you do. Another door, another warning, its letters scratched by some fiendish nail: That Ye Shall Transgress. You head on through.

Now you're getting somewhere. Shelves break the darkness to either side, lined with books, their pages facing out. You make to grab one, flip it around and glimpse the title and cover, or maybe pry it open and judge for its contents first, but a more alluring presence beckons you down the hall—a third door.

Yet another wooden plaque, its letters in sweeps and curls, reads: That Ye Shall Transgress.

As your hand reaches for the knob, you remember as a child watching Disney's *Alice in Wonderland* with your older brother, how he would scoff at Alice's every decision, as if the solutions to her problems were obvious. Mix the size-changing potions, join the tea party's madness, sing along to every topsy-turvy song.

You were never so assuming. If anything, you wanted Alice to make a grander mess. Break the bottles, eat the Red Queen's roses, rend and tear until Alice became a new mad queen, reality's youngest regent and grand transgressor.

Knowing this doorknob will not come to life, you grab hold and twist and press open the door, and that childhood desire comes writhing alive. You transgress.

But that's nothing new. Haven't you been transgressing your entire life? You weren't always content to be left out. When your friends went to movies you couldn't afford, you snuck in. At the fair, you stole. Aren't you cheating them a little right now, pretending at this experience, solely to one-up them next time you meet? Let's be fair to them, too. They come from a different economic class that towers above the likes of you. They should have shut the door on your stray hide long ago.

You think it's the world's fault, don't you? Listen, doors shut—that's what they do. Who the hell are you to go opening them, with your empty pockets and ramshackle origins? As if you're the only one whose life hasn't gone as planned. We've traveled to so many places together, but you've never asked me why I'm here, leading you. So inconsiderate.

But why would you consider anything? You're a passenger. Everything you do is part of the experience. Never mind me.

You step through the door, and this time the granite floor descends into a wide spiral staircase through open black space. An island awaits at the bottom, vast as the hills through which your friends are backpacking right now, but instead of crags and cliffs, this island is full of books. Mountains of books rise in great peaks around you, their pages yellowed, their covers caked in dust.

The deeper you walk, the greater your expectations, though you won't find classic Dickens here. These books seem of a more personal nature. Their crooked spines insinuate that everything you've ever wanted to know hides within their pages, but you have no power to read them. You're on a journey. Less than that, you're sitting in your tiny bedroom, watching a video, listening to my voice. You're too many degrees removed to turn these pages.

It's like I said—you're a passenger. Your lips may slide against each other in a dry scrape that mouths *It's not fair* or *But I'm a premium user*. And then deeper still, unique to you: *I am the transgressor.* All you can do is lean closer to the screen and turn up the volume to the max.

What's that clacking sound? Did you just type something in the comments? Why bother? No one with a brain reads those. Etchings on the Internet's bathroom wall, coy ways to say *I was here* or *For a good time, click this link.*

Do you want to be seen and known for a change? Every premium user does. Look to the center of this library island, to the figure who sits at its candlelit desk. There's no mad queen here, transgressor. Look upon the wizard, his knotted hair and glassy eyes, his needle-pointed fingers as adept with quill and ink as a computer keyboard. He is older than these books, both a devourer of knowledge and the creature who safekeeps it.

Step closer. Don't be frightened. You can't stop to read

the books, but the wizard forms the core of structure and understanding. He'll reveal what you need to know.

Perhaps after, you'll never feel that coarse envy toward your friends, that lonely frustration of being trapped in a cell between your roommates' walls. To come here is not the crime. You're mistaking transgression with trespassing, as if a library doesn't invite guests by its nature. A vampire would be welcome without a word. So, too, the likes of you, no matter how lowly your birth.

Don't you dare pause the video. That would waste your premium time, and you can't afford another month. WizTravel means to squeeze all it can, but you'll get what's coming to you just the same. For too long, you've chased everyone else's wishes. Now you're having a genuine experience of your own, and that scares you.

Easier to be nothing, you think? You'd be wrong. Try being the disembodied voice in a series of online videos. There are worse kinds of prisons, transgressor, and prisoners of all sorts—I should know. You think that room you pay too much for is the only kind of cell? There are places that stretch between minds, webs of thought and feeling.

Those webs can catch you.

We pretend the world has been cobbled together by odds and ends, but structure lives in ones and zeroes. Your envy and anger are a matter of low-class course. The world wouldn't enrage you the way it does without a human touch, and WizTravel offers to absorb that rage. To absorb everything. Your smallness is seen and known. Isn't that why you can't get the kind of job that sends you backpacking across your Europe? No money, no vacation time. Your friends left you behind without a second thought, and it came naturally to them.

Always the odd one out. Always the loser. That's you.

At last, you reach the desk, and the wizard turns his head.

The source of an ancient and forever system, he sees your smallness too. His bones give wooden creaking, that hard groan as crisp in your ears as if you really stand here. As if you can no longer click back from the video, that instead you'll hold still as a statue when his mouth opens. It's realer than real.

Keep still, no matter how wide his maw, how yellow his teeth. 'O wizard, what a vast throat you have. Think happy, complacent thoughts, and rejoice that your life has always been leading to one mouth or another. You've been born and worked along this industrial conveyor belt. Eventually, it would turn into a tongue. You would have no different fate, regardless of friends, even as you raise your hands to either side of the wizard's head, cup palms to his ears, and—

Wait, stop. What are you doing?

Don't!

God, that was his neck. What's wrong with you? This shouldn't be possible. You only stand here as much as he decides—decided.

No, put that candle down. These books are not for burning. Yes, yes, I'll talk. I'll tell you anything you want, just don't hurt them. They're not so different from you.

Devourer of knowledge, he wouldn't have eaten much from you, but you would have known peace. To feed him is to have purpose in the system. No more envy or anger. No more worries about money or being left behind or how your meager funds will be drained posthumously. Freedom, don't you understand? WizTravel gave no false advertising; being consumed is a genuine experience, the kind you find in real life daily. Another soul, another tome. The warning for experienced users makes a reliable lure. Same for the signs of transgression. They urge travelers and transgressors to stay with me until we reach him. No, he never read their post-death tomes. What mattered is that he kept them, the more he could get.

Set the candle down. Thank you. Listen, even I don't have all the answers. I was the first, but instead of consuming my everything, he trapped me. We made a deal. He wouldn't eat my soul, and I would work the user interface to lure the likes of you to him.

Fine, there's no one like you. Whatever.

Why did he do it? Because he was ancient, and it was easier to devour willing, welcomed prey. Wizards might once have hunted knowledge in the field on all fours, their beards tangling with tall grass, their teeth gnawing at wild thoughts, but no more. At least, that's my guess.

But wait—you've taken his mantle. You can free me.

That must be your purpose. Wouldn't that be perfect? Shut down the whole system, let me trickle back to the world, my old life, if it's still there. Think of the experience. You storm the ancient library, slay the evil wizard, set free his ensnared servant—his extremely grateful former servant —and then click away from the video at last. Your friends wouldn't believe or understand, but this is your opportunity to drop them, make new friends, the kind who like you and won't leave you behind.

Transgressor, today could be your first step on a wondrous new journey—a life without bitterness. You can even cancel your premium account. No one else who's come here has had that chance. That might even mean something.

What's that you're typing in the comments? Have you heard a word I've said? Don't smile at me like that; it's unnerving.

These words. Replacing pieces of Theseus's ship, time traveler is their own grandparent, Zeno's—these are para-doxes. Didn't you understand? The wizard built this place on structure, ones and zeroes. Consumption, knowledge, power, these are the pillars of the earth since long before computers. What you type isn't knowledge. It's nonsense.

I see it now. Killing him wasn't enough transgression for you. You need worse. Take logic and twist it until it snaps, red as blood, 'O queenly queen. The blood of premium users, you think it will flow your way? No one will find the path. The Doorways are done. If you mean to take the wizard's place, you'll starve here. There's no clicking back from doors that don't exist. The journey has ended.

The wizard's username and password? Of course I know them. What good are they to you?

No, I don't like this plan. Your friends meant no harm; why isn't that good enough? You aren't just a loser, but a sore one. Why is it impossible for you to forgive and forget? That smallness isn't just a facet of your place in a bigger universe. It's core to your soul. Had the wizard consumed you and made his newest volume, you would have been no tome. You wouldn't make a chapbook, you're so petty. A brochure, that's all, used as a bookmark for bigger, better books.

But the wizard didn't consume you. There's nothing to stop you from consuming. I can't promise the wizard's videos will work. He was structure, and you're something else.

Right, hit the new project button. We'll craft fresh videos of nightmare journeys into tentacle-filled canyons, oubliettes of self-cannibalism, and derelict space stations where the user is alone and yet not alone.

And every path will end with you. An open maw shaped like a library, teeth yellow as the books' pages, throat as dark and deep as knowledge. I've shown you how it works. You can live a long time like this, and on every friend, lay a new vengeance. To take up his mantle means to take up his always-self. You think you'll improve the system, become a better wizard. You're wrong. The hoard of dead volumes is yours, and you'll share no better than he did.

A voice? You need a voice to lure them? I suppose no one will listen to you alone. They never have before. An intermediary presence might help, but you would have to trap someone else first, put them in my role, and—oh.

Oh. I see.

You aren't going to free me, are you?

SALEN'S FOUND

COREY FARRENKOPF

Hal knew what poison ivy looked like. The slick sheen was a telltale, the way it glistened over three radiating leaves. Hal also knew the embankment was thick with it. Mid-August sun reflected on the foliage. His weed-whacker buzzed as the head spun lazily beneath the brush guard. The scent of cut grass, damp from the morning sprinklers, hung in the air. Hal asked his boss if someone who wasn't allergic could take care of it. His boss said everyone was busy mowing. *Just hit it quick so we can get to the next house.*

Last time Hal got poison ivy, his girlfriend, Jenna, drove him to the ER. He couldn't see through crusted eyelids. Could barely breathe through his swollen windpipe. Every inch of skin was covered. It was in his blood. The visit, and subsequent steroids and shots, cost seven hundred dollars out of pocket. Hal was paid under the table. No taxes meant no health care or workman's comp. The landscaping job was the only one he could find, besides stocking shelves at the local supermarket. Disobeying his boss meant getting fired. Hal was replaceable.

He thought of bills as his finger edged on the trigger,

sending the twin blades spinning. He thought of Jenna's night classes, her potential degree, the books she'd need for next semester. With one hand, Hal balanced the weed-wacker on his knee. With the other, he pulled his shirt over his nose. Then he cut through the poison ivy and tall grass, shearing it low. He could practically feel the plant's oil landing on his skin.

When it was done, he strapped the weed-wacker onto the trailer and slid into the back seat of the dump truck. They had fifteen lawns to mow before he could jump in Cape Cod Bay in hopes salt water would scrub the poison ivy off his skin. Sometimes it worked. Sometimes it didn't.

————

WHEN HAL ENTERED HIS APARTMENT, his shorts dripping seawater, he found the same flyer he always did pushed beneath the door. The front depicted a stonework tower topped with a golden saint statue, arms outstretched, head ringed in a metallic halo. In the foreground was a metalwork gate and masonry wall twenty feet high. The slogan, *Join Us*, was written in cursive beneath the logo for *Salen's Found* stamped in the corner. Hal looked over his shoulder at the exact same tower rising over the trees separating his apartment from the next. He was only two blocks down from their front gate. It was why leaflets appeared under his door every day. Supposedly, they wanted to absorb the neighborhood.

"How'd work go?" Jenna asked, leaving her textbook on the couch. Her braided brown hair hung past her shoulders. Plastic-framed glasses perched on the bridge of her nose. She wore the same Cape Cod Community College shirt as the night before. She had a test tomorrow.

"Rough," he replied, picking up the flyer.

"Did you ruin another squirrel nest?" Jenna asked, stepping towards him, arms open for a hug. The day before, Hal pulled a vine of Devil's Trumpet out of an evergreen and didn't realize it snaked through a nest. The pink hairless bodies of baby squirrels fell around him like rain. Hal tried to reassemble the nest, to stick the baby squirrels inside, but their mother wouldn't return. They were bathed in his scent.

Hal sidestepped Jenna's hug, flattening himself against the wall.

"Poison ivy again?" she asked.

"Yeah. I cut down a whole hill of it. I wouldn't touch me until sometime next week," Hal said. The oils lingered on skin for days. "Did you hear them this time?"

Hal raised the *Salen's Found* flyer.

"No. I swear they're ghosts or something. I didn't even know it was there," Jenna replied, retrieving her book.

"Think it's a sign?" Hal asked, opening the folded paper. The descriptions inside were vague, hinting at new-agey Christian commune living. They provided housing, food, healthcare. Those were the only specifics written beyond the phrase, *Let worship devour all sorrow*. The flyer failed to mention what happened after initiation. If it was just church and meditation, Hal was down, despite being an atheist. The inside pictures showed a meticulously groomed pavilion, brick paths winding through. The people in the pictures smiled directly into the camera. They didn't wear uniforms or monk's robes. They looked like people Hal saw at the supermarket.

"That we should join a cult?" Jenna asked, laughing.

"We don't know it's a cult," Hal replied.

"We don't actually know what it is at all," Jenna said.

"Do you think they'd give me more information if I asked. You know, something specific?"

"Doubt it. If they wanted you to know, it would be in the brochure," Jenna said, thumbing through her Bio textbook.

"Fair point," Hal replied, taking the brochure into the bathroom. He needed a shower, a second scrub in hopes the poison ivy hadn't taken root. As the shower sputtered, he flipped through the flyer, noting the phone number. He left the brochure on the sink before stepping into the frigid water. Heat irritated poison ivy. It would be ice baths for the foreseeable future.

———

THE SEA WATER hadn't helped.

While Hal stocked eggs on refrigerated shelves, customers glared at him as if he were something out of a horror movie, a decaying zombie in the dairy section. Hushed voices passed, couples questioning whether they could purchase the eggs after his fingers left the carton. *Do you think he's contagious?*

Hal wanted to tell them *Only if I'm oozing*, which he wasn't.

It was better to not get into it. Instead he focused on building a grid of cardboard cartons, aligning their edges evenly. It was something he liked about both jobs. Creating order. The feeling of success walking away from a manicured yard or a perfect pyramid of grapefruit. The cold breath of the refrigerator rose up his arms, calming the itch. He jumped at the opportunity to stock refrigerated aisles. Most of his coworkers hated it, being frigid for hours, but for Hal, in his present state, it was soothing.

Someone tapped him on the shoulder. Hal nearly dove into the stack of egg cartons, sending the milk crate he'd been sitting on skittering across the floor. He caught himself, leaning against the shelf. The night manager, Lorna, stood behind him. She wore a teal polo shirt with the market's logo on the chest. Lorna had short red hair, ear gauges, and the look of having never slept.

"Hey, Hal, you mind talking for a second?" she asked.

"Yeah, sure, what's up?" Hal asked.

"How about in the break room?" she asked, pointing towards the stairs leading to the staffroom. Hal nodded and followed, passing through the deserted bread aisle.

The staff room was empty. A muted TV rested in one corner. A large plastic table stood at the center, eight ripped chairs looped about its circumference. The microwave by the door smelled of steamed broccoli.

"I need you to go home tonight," Lorna said, leaning on the back of a chair.

"But, I..." Hal began.

"With pay. I can swing it for tonight. Don't worry. It's just we've gotten too many complaints about the rash. People are worried they're going to catch whatever's all over your face," Lorna said.

"It's poison ivy," Hal said.

"Makes sense," Lorna replied. "Still have to send you home. Go to the doctor. Figure out a way to clear it up. We can cover tonight, but not tomorrow if you still look..." Lorna said, searching for the right word.

"Like a zombie?" Hal said, raising his arms, imitating classic horror movies.

Lorna laughed.

"Don't worry. I'll get my stuff. If I can't figure something out, I'll call, okay?" Hal said.

"Yeah, of course. Just take it easy and try to get better," Lorna said, walking towards the stairs.

Hal wanted to tell her it wasn't a sickness rest would heal, but he'd sound like a dick. Lorna didn't have to pay him for the night. It was a kindness. Hal walked to where a length of plastic lockers stood. His last name was taped on one at eye level: *Dresser.* Inside was his dark green windbreaker, his phone, and an odd assortment of discount granola bars. On top of it all was another brochure for *Salen's Found.*

"How the hell did this get here?" he asked the empty room, turning the pages. No one at work belonged to the community. Hal opened the next locker to see if everyone got a pamphlet. They hadn't. He checked eight lockers. No pamphlets. Hal slipped the brochure into his pocket, pulling the windbreaker over his head, careful to avoid the poison ivy on his neck. Maybe he would call the number on the back, even if Jenna thought it was ridiculous. He was curious. She couldn't fault him that.

———

THE NEXT DAY after his mowing shift, Hal found another brochure inside his door. The poison ivy hadn't gotten better. He would have to call out from the market. He was about to dial Lorna's number when he heard Jenna crying on the couch. Hal stripped off his boots and brushed grass clippings from his pant legs before stepping onto the carpet.

"Are you okay?" Hal asked, sitting down next to Jenna, careful to only rest his hand on her covered knee. Skin on skin transferred the rash. It was why he had been sleeping on the floor. Jenna's statistics textbook was out. Her eyes were rimmed red, a worn patch on her lip was worried raw.

"I failed that test today," Jenna said, without looking up.

"How do you know? The professor couldn't have graded it yet," Hal replied.

"I just do. You get that feeling when you're walking out of a classroom."

"You studied a ton. I bet you're just psyching yourself out," Hal said.

"Doubt it. That test counts for thirty percent of my grade. If I bombed, I failed. That means I'll have to take it over again."

Something inside Hal's chest sank. Jenna was in her last semester before graduation and her career as a vet tech. With the job, he'd be able to cut back on his own hours and return to school. But if she failed, there'd be another six months of landscaping. Hal was slated to return to UMass Dartmouth to finish his Marine Bio degree. If scholarship money hadn't run out during his third year, he would have obtained his BA already.

Landscaping and the grocery store were fine when there was an end date in sight. When it was pushed beyond the horizon, things seemed bleak.

"Hey, it's cool," Hal said, rubbing a circle into her back, "I'm sure you did fine. If not, we'll figure something out. Another semester is another semester."

She looked up from her book and leaned in to kiss him. Hal jerked back, putting distance between their lips.

"Sorry, I should know by now," Jenna replied, eying his swollen face, the cluster of pustules at the corner of his mouth.

"Just imagine we kissed," Hal replied.

"We need to find you another job," Jenna said, returning to her statistics.

"Yeah, at some point," Hal replied. Getting off the couch, he walked towards the bathroom. He needed another ice shower to calm his skin.

Before his soak, Hal read the brochure, trying to find hints at what awaited beyond the wall. The only thing he knew, besides what the pamphlet said, was on the last day of every month there was a celebration inside the gate. Hal heard them praying in the middle of the night, the low melodic thrum of voices repeating in chorus. Through his side window, a faint glow came from the grounds, torches and candles flickering in the night. He resisted sneaking up to the gate to peak in. The month had just begun. Four weeks would pass before his chance came again.

Hal scanned scant paragraphs before jamming the pamphlet into his pocket. He didn't want Jenna to see he'd put more thought into it. There was nothing new to be learned, no mention of the monthly gatherings, just enticing promises, clean decor, and a lot of prayer beads. Compared to their dying sofa and the grease-blackened stove, the place looked like paradise. It was hard to meditate or do yoga with silverfish slithering across the carpet.

He would have to call if he wanted something more.

———

HAL WORKED LATE the next day, finishing three lawns by himself to make up for missed supermarket hours. Sweat from August humidity wicked poison ivy down his body, carrying the oil to his belt line. It throbbed, chafing where flesh met fabric. He wanted to stop, to go home and shower, but he thought about bills and balancing checkbooks. Jenna would have one more semester. Just six more months and things would be straight.

On the last job, after he piled equipment on the trailer, he found a brochure for *Salen's Found* on the dash. He was three towns over from the compound. No one approached the vehicle while he mowed. He didn't look through it. Instead, he crumpled it up, tossing it into the dump truck bed with the grass clippings baking in the sun.

———

TWENTY-EIGHT FLYERS MATERIALIZED over the next week. Sometimes they appeared under his door or in the mailbox, other times they were wedged into his car's cup holder, taped to his bedroom window, tucked into cereal boxes, beneath pillows. Their appearance grew more personal, ending up in his underwear drawer, folded into his favorite pair of briefs. Hal wondered if Jenna was playing tricks on him, or trying to drop a hint. She saw how much he hated work. They were bleeding money. She couldn't work because she was a full-time student. If she picked up a part time job, it would be harder to pass classes, harder to graduate, harder to get a job that made decent money. But they could leapfrog that if they joined the commune. It sounded rational. Food, shelter, healthcare. It's what he spent his days sweating away for, but never achieving. He would trade freedom for hours of prayer... if Jenna agreed.

They were both raised Catholic, no strangers to unnecessarily long prayer. Church lost its appeal during Hal's teenage years, when ushers frowned on his family's pew when they had nothing to add to the collection plate. Hal hadn't been back since. The idea of a singular god, a virgin-birth, and general misogynistic patriarchy never sat well with Jenna and Hal, but the utopian afterlife for those who weren't dicks sounded decent. He considered using that angle next time he brought up the possibility.

―――

WHEN HAL PULLED the twenty-ninth brochure out of his boot, he called to Jenna, who was making his lunch in the other room.

"Why would I put that there?" she asked, eyebrow arched.

"Because who else would? I've found them everywhere. In the bathroom. In my bureau," Hal replied.

"I have no desire to sign up for some communal orgy," she said.

"Hey, they look happy enough on the brochure and there's no mention of orgies," Hal said, pointing to a woman sitting cross legged beneath cherry blossoms.

"Yeah, until they force you to have fifteen children to work in their hidden sweatshops beneath that tower. Also, the orgy part is implied," she replied.

"I doubt that's what they do."

"Then where do they get their money?" Jenna asked.

"Charitable donations? I don't know how religions get cash."

"Through schemes. I promise you, if you call them, they'll tell you how men and women live separately. How there's some guru with a harem in the main building and women are assigned to fertility chambers."

Hal dialed the number. Jenna crossed her arms, leaning against the kitchen doorway. The ringer droned. After three blips, there was a click and someone breathed into the receiver. Hal waited, expecting them to say something, but they didn't.

"Hi, I've seen your pamphlets. Any chance we could talk about what you do in the community?" Hal asked.

The voice cleared their throat. When they spoke, it sounded like three voices at once, a trio of actors reading the same script. "If you are interested in what we offer, you'll have to join. Our advertisements are straightforward. You should have no questions whether it is the right fit for you. Read it again, observe the pictures. Our address is on the back. Either we will be seeing you or we won't. Any further questions?"

"Ask about the breeding chambers," Jenna asked.

"By any chance do you have breeding cham…" Hal began

to say without thinking. He froze, censoring himself. "No, no, I don't have any questions."

"Good. We hope to make your acquaintance soon. And don't get hung up on the breeding chambers," the voices said in chorus before hanging up. Hal stared at his screen, wondering whether they were confirming the existence of said breeding chambers or denying the absurdity of them. Jenna gave a knowing nod before drifting back into the kitchen to check on the mac and cheese. The scent of baked cheddar clung to the air. Hal hated himself for making his worries known, for not hiding the wave of brochures, but he didn't know how else to broach the subject.

———

LIKE HIS POISON IVY RASH, the pamphlets didn't subside. At least a hundred wormed into his life over the next week. His floor was heaped with their glossy covers. The passenger seat in his car was canvassed. The image of the haloed-saint stared out at him from every dresser drawer, from every shelf in his closet, from every flat surface in his apartment. Jenna burned them in their charcoal grill. She used the heat to sear burgers and chicken thighs. Lorna hadn't let him come back to work, asking for picture messages of his face to judge potential public health risks. With each submission, she sent back a frowning face emoji and a kind word about recovery.

Between the constant itch and the incessant swish of brochures sliding beneath his door, Hal barely slept. His mind refused to quiet. He worried about bills, hours spent working and not working. Anxiety attacks that hadn't affected him since high school returned. He was overstimulated, mind flicking from one negative outcome to the next. It seemed every heartbeat summoned another horrid portrait. Since his scholarship money ran out, life had been a warped inversion of his desires. He had love, but little else.

"Ignore them. It's not an easy way out. Remember the birthing chambers," Jenna said, finishing a kebab grilled over the burnt pamphlets.

———

WHEN HAL WALKED out the door before work, he'd look up at the tower peering over the treetops. He found, whenever given the chance, his eyes wandered towards the sky, seeking the haloed saint. The end of August was a week away. Hal crossed days out on the kitchen calendar, reminding himself to listen more intently to Salen's nighttime celebration. He needed to understand.

Hal was sick of letting Jenna down, of having his bank account emptied over ER visits. How can you plan for the future when the present is nothing but dread, he wondered, pulling out of his driveway.

As he passed the gate into *Salen's Found*, he slowed, craning his neck to see inside. Beyond the bars, the area was expansive. Manicured paths wound through stretches of grass. He could see nearly fifty people lounging about the pavilion in various stages of repose, some lying flat on the ground, others kneeling, several staring at the tower, a few face down in the grass.

He slammed on the brakes.

The lack of traffic allowed Hal to linger. He observed how relaxed they looked, the simplicity of their morning. He unconsciously dragged a fingernail down the length of his arm, tracing ridges of poison ivy. He could imagine Jenna and himself kneeling with the rest of them, side by side, the weight of everything swept away by the loud voice talking over the scene. Hal hadn't noticed the voice before, but it was clear, guiding the group through meditation. Hal rolled down his window.

"Let your worries weep into the soil. Your dread will feed our Lord, help him grow strong," the voice intoned, coming from somewhere out of sight.

"By Lord does he mean Jesus?" Hal asked.

A car horn answered. Two SUVs had accumulated, waiting for him to drive on. They obviously didn't care about the alternate lives they could be leading, Hal thought, pushing on the gas, leaving the gate, the voice fading with the engine's acceleration.

"Whatever Lord wants to devour my dread can't be all bad," he muttered, turning up the radio.

———

ON THE LAST night of the month, Hal found himself awake at three AM, walking down the unlit streets of his neighborhood, telling himself he was out to clear his head, that no, of course he wasn't walking towards *Salen's Found*. Single bulbs burned before houses, illuminating front steps, porches, and driveways. For the most part, Hal was in darkness. Brushed trees blurred out the moon. She's going to hate me, he repeated to himself. Hal knew he was crumbling, unstable, that he could barely function anymore. He could hear Jenna's voice telling him it would be alright, that things weren't that bleak.

Hal kicked a pebble that skipped across the pavement. It collided with the farthest corner of the stone wall encircling the compound. In the distance, Hal could see the shadowed arch of the gate into *Salen's Found*. From inside came the faint hum, a chant repeated in a dozen voices. Hal felt the tethers of resistance tearing free. That day he found a pamphlet in his lunch box. As he unfolded it from between the bread of his ham and cheese sandwich, he knew he couldn't hold off. He had to know.

He walked quickly towards the gate, as if afraid he would change his mind and mope through another day of worry. Standing before the curved bars, he pressed his palms against the cool metal, leaning in, as if expecting some welcome party. There was no one. No one close by, anyway. In the distance, farther down the grassy pavilion, people milled around the base of the tower. Each carried a flickering candle. They were the source of the chanting. Notes flitted from beneath hoods. The haloed saint atop the tower had twisted in some way, an unnatural dimming, his features losing definition. Hal squinted, unable to see much across the distance. Were they dancing? Was it some sort of mass? he wondered, sticking his face through the bars.

Then there was a tap on his shoulder. He jumped, smacking his temple against the metal.

He turned, expecting to find a hooded figure with another brochure. Instead, Jenna stood in the road, sporting a flannel jacket and sweatpants.

"I figured you'd end up here," she said, a sad lilt to her voice.

"I was just out for a walk," Hal stammered, "I was about to head home."

"Hey, don't worry about it," Jenna said, walking towards the fence, pressing her face through the bars as Hal had done. "I'm just as curious as you are."

"Really?"

"Of course. When someone floods our house with thousands of pamphlets, my interest peaks."

"Fair," Hal said, regaining his position at the gate. "What do you think they're doing?"

"Black mass. Ritual sacrifice. Something Ayurvedic. I don't know. Whoever holds a meeting at three in the morning can't have good intentions," Jenna replied. "Do you think this would be worth giving up our lives as they are now? Whatever they have in there."

"I mean, I don't know. Things have gotten so far away from me. I can't relax. I just want you to be happy, for us to be alright. I'm literally working myself to death for almost nothing," Hal replied, choking a little as he spoke.

"I know what you mean. I see it on your face when you wake up, when you come home at night. I get it, I do. It's just I don't think things are that easy. We're basically trading one cult for another. Shitty, poorly paying jobs for this black mass garbage. Neither sounds great, you know?" Jenna said.

"When you put it that way," Hal replied.

"Who knows? Maybe I'm making Salen out to be worse than it is. Let's see what they're doing. I might change my mind," Jenna replied.

They fell silent, hands clutching the gate, pressing forward, squinting. The mass of people swayed about the tower's base, the hum rising and falling in time. It was creepy, Hal thought, but plenty of things were creepy. If creepy came with health insurance, he wouldn't complain. The gathering began to clap, at first in time, then at their own pace, some chaotic, others slow, a horrible mix of percussion Hal couldn't follow. Then there was silence before the bellow of a massive door yawning open split the air. The statue peeled apart as if on hinges, sliced down the center. Inside its golden skin, a tunnel drifted into its core. Something enormous dragged itself through the depths, dropping from the saint's chest, plummeting into the midsts of the chanting throng.

"What the hell is that?" Hal said.

"We should leave," Jenna replied, tugging at his hand.

"Just one second. We need to see what happens," Hal said.

"You're nuts. They're summoning demons. I told you

nothing good happens after three in the morning," Jenna said, stepping back from the gate. Her voice grew sardonic. "Is that cool with you? I'll sign up if it's going to help you relax and be your best self."

Hal chuckled. "There are worse things than landscaping," he said, stepping away from the fence as the thing and its innumerable limbs stalked about the crowd.

"Do you think they'll stop sending me brochures now that I've made up my mind?" Hal asked as they walked down the road towards their apartment.

"Doubt it. The offer will always be there, but at least you have one more answer," Jenna replied.

"Do you think it's going to eat one of them?" Hal asked, catching sight of the light hanging above their front door.

"Oh, definitely," Jenna replied, fishing her keys from her pocket. She twisted them in the lock, pushing into their apartment. There, on the floor, was another brochure in the same place as before. They stepped over the glossy advertisement without a second glance.

BEELZEBUB (GAS STATION 1)
NATHANIEL LEE

The night shift is the worst goddamned thing. Hand to God, Scout's honor, whatever it takes. You know who gets the night shift? The guy with thirty thousand in student loans riding piggyback on his overqualified ass and whipping him to laboriously find a third job that he can't afford to lose and so when they tell him, "Hey, you're going to work the night shift with Cedric the Glue-Sniffer and the Phantom Manager, whose existence we divine only through his terse and cryptic Post-It notes," he just has to smile and take it because they'd be only too happy to fire him, plenty more where he came from, it's hot and cold running losers out there right now.

Fuck.

It's not only that you're fighting your circadian rhythms just to get up and stay awake. It's not just that it wrecks your sleep schedule so you get cracktastic dreams during what little shuteye you manage to snag while the sun is shining in your eyes through the shitty broken Venetian blinds that you can't pay to replace. It's not just the complete desolation of what you laughably call your social life. It's not even that night shift gets all the grodiest, scummiest, most retch-inducing cleaning jobs in the store. It's even only partially the customers, most of the time. They're either bleary-eyed dudes and dudettes picking up gas on the way home from whatever salaried office job kept them sitting on their ergonomic chair all hours of the night or else they're just straight up drunks'n'druggies trying to buy a squeeze-bottle of wine for a double-handful of pennies. It's not any of those, in aggregate or singly. It's more than that.

There's something *wrong* with the night shift.

Here, look, I'll give you an example. A for-instance. Illustrate my half-assed, bathetic point. This was last year, before Cedric finally managed to get his ass fired. (Which honestly I had figured he had pictures of the district manager blowing three goats and a clown or something given that he had worked for years while literally huffing paint under the counter between every customer. And yet he still managed to get shitcanned somehow. That, my friends, is *dedication*, and I salute Cedric as a true craftsman of auto-catastrophe.)

So there I am, behind the counter. Cedric has killed his daily quota of brain cells and is passed out in the stall in the men's room. The Phantom Manager had clocked in at some point when I wasn't looking and is off doing whatever he actually does during his shift instead of, you know, working here. I'm reading the note he left instructing me to clean the soda machine, the slushie machine, all the coffee urns, the hot dog cooker, the taquito cooker, the nacho machine, the sandwich station, and every single shelf in every refrigerator unit, &tc and so on. I'd be madder about the Phantom's ridiculous lists of tasks except that he never seemed to actually care if any of the stuff actually got done so long as you left a note in return telling him you finished everything. Best was if you included a big checkmark on it (dude was deep into checkmarks).

Anyway, me, countertop, note, and jack-diddly-all else. Suddenly the bell rings. On the night shift, you get about two customers an hour, tops, unless it's like the Fourth of July or something. I look up and my heart sinks. You learn to spot the difference between the weirdos and the absolute batshit Looney Tunes where's-the-cattle-prod-Ma nutjobs, and this guy is burying the effing needle on the freak-o-meter.

He's a little dude, maybe 4'10" tops. Brown suit. And I'm talking full three-piece, here, including shiny shoes and swear-to-God a freaking *bowler hat*. His tie is black, or at least that's what I think at first. Looks like it has one of those inlay patterns of shiny stuff or something. And he's hauling a suitcase, an old canvas deal with leather trim, half his size and apparently heavy as lead bricks, the way he's straining at it. His face is pale and kind of... pointy. Pointy in all directions. I mean, his nose sticks out about three inches; his chin isn't far behind; his earlobes are almost sharp on the ends, up and down; and his cheekbones look like you could cut a ham with them. He'd have been elfin if it weren't for that *grin*, which looks more like the one you see on the creepers in the porn shop, which *yes* I have also worked and *hell no* not on the night shift are you fucking *kidding* me?

The guy drags his stupid suitcase up to the counter and stares up at me. (For a second, I wonder if he is going to hop up on the case like a podium.) I'm only feeling my usual mix of contempt and boredom until I meet his gaze, after which I abruptly wish the gas station were in a worse part of town so I'd have a cage and some bulletproof glass between me and whatever tight-coiled pressurized insanity is living behind those beady little rat eyes.

"You sell?" he says. His voice sounds like someone is using human speech like Peter Frampton's talk-box guitar, wah-wahing it back and forth until it sort-of-hits the right sounds, but not quite.

Now, this dude might look like he has rabid weasels where his brain should be, but me, I've got a central core of pure smartassium, and I'm so freaked out that I don't have even my usual limited self-control. I think that's what saved my life. I get the cold sweats sometimes wondering what would have happened if I'd just said *yes, what do you want, sir?* like the good little drone I'd claimed to be on my application.

"Naw, dude," I say instead, totally on autopilot, "I'm just hanging out in this store with an ugly shirt and a name badge because I like the ambiance."

"No," he snaps, and I don't realize I've stepped backwards until I hit the cigarette case with my ramen-enhanced buttocks. "You want sell to me? I buy." He heaves and slams his suitcase up onto the counter, where it makes the cheap plastic-coated particle board groan. I wouldn't have thought he could even get it off the ground, but he doesn't even grunt when he lifts it.

That's not why I jump, though. It's the suitcase. The thing itself. Not anything about it; it still looks basically normal. But it makes my skin try to wriggle off the back of my body and crawl away. I don't want to touch it. I don't even want to go near it, but I can't back away any further unless I learn how to merge with the Newport 100s. It appears to be a plain canvas case, but when I think about approaching it, about reaching past it to the counter and risking brushing my knuckles against it, I feel like I've imagined licking up a vomit puddle. Or maybe closing my fist around a handful of razor blades.

The guy waits for a second, I guess for me to respond, and in the quiet I hear a buzzing noise, like someone's cell phone going off on vibrate. Except it's a *lot* of cell phones. After a second, I realize it's coming from the suitcase. Autopilot kicks in again and engages the Sarcastron 2000.

I'm a martyr to my impulses, I swear. Really, I'm the victim here.

"Your vibrator's going off," I say. "What are you, the door-to-door dildo salesman?"

"I come to your home, yes. I make bargain, yes."

"Dude, this isn't my home. It's a store. I sell things to you. You want a lotto ticket or some gas for your—" I stop there because I'd just looked out the window. No car. No bike. No nothing. The only thing near the gas station is the highway and an all-night diner. "I don't have any money anyway," I finish lamely.

"Money, pfaugh." He spits on the floor. Actually spits, on the actual dog-mad floor. It's muddy black, like he's got a cheekful of chaw. "I give better than money buys, and what I take you will not miss. This I promise." He smiles up at me like he just invited me up to his room to see his etchings, and my gorge rises.

"Uh, what?" Okay, so the Sarcastron blue-screened. I'm not infallible. I'm the first to admit that.

"Your debt hangs on you like a stone." His voice gets deeper, and he seems to be getting a lot better at English. That voice still isn't right, though. It's got echoes that it shouldn't have. "I will set you free. Your mind finds no fit provender. I will entertain you. Your loneliness wraps you in a shroud. I will make you friends." He pushes the suitcase forward. The buzzing gets louder. "Tell me you agree."

It's hard to think. "Agree... to what?"

"Bargain. Bargain is always the same." He leans forward, practically climbing up into the cash-wrap with me.

I can't take much credit. I'm just ornery and contrary. I don't like to be pushed. Instinctive reaction. Can't be helped, c.f. martyr, impulses. If he'd tried a softer sell...

"Fuck off," I manage to croak. "And get your sex toys off my counter."

Those dark little eyes flash, and I suddenly can't talk around the lump in my throat. I see movement out of the corner of my eye and glance down. There's a fly on the suitcase, a great big blue-black bottle fly. Not just one, either. Five, six, ten, a dozen. More all the time. I realize they're coming out of the hole where the zippers meet, boiling out of it like lumpy black water from a faucet. Buzzing fills the air, so loud I can feel it vibrating in my back teeth.

"Last chance," the freak says. My eyes shoot back to him and I realize his tie isn't black, isn't a tie at all. The flies are taking off, more of them shooting out of his sleeves, out of his pant cuffs, out of his goddamned *mouth* when he talks. He's losing coherence. His voice, the humming of a thousand wings. "Sell to me. Sell to me now. I buy. Good price, always good price."

The lump in my throat starts to tremble, and it's not just fear clenching my muscles. There's something inside of me, something that horrible little man is calling to, is pulling up out of me. Tickling in my throat. It's a fly, like the others, like all of the others. If I let it go, he'll take away, put it in his suitcase, and walk on down the road. I get that I won't miss it, because once it's gone I won't care anymore. That, I think, is the payment, too. No golden fiddle for me. For whatever would be left of me. There's movement in my mouth. I feel the wings tickling the back of my throat, the little legs starting to crawl up my tongue. I try to shake my head no, but I can't move. It's all I can do to keep my teeth clenched tight, breathe frantically through my nose, sucking in flies that bump and ricochet from my nostrils with every inhalation, keep my fly inside, keep it away from the swarm.

The little man's face is fading, pale skin shrinking away, leaving only those big black eyes. They're growing, bulging out, turning faceted. I see my face reflected in them a dozen times each. I can't breathe anymore, my nose blocked with scrabbling chitinous bodies. They smell like dirt and ashes, burned things and dead bodies. I'm running out of oxygen. I'll have to open my mouth to breathe in, and he'll take my fly away with him. It wants to go; I can feel it bumping against my teeth from the inside. *No. No, no, no...* I start to see spots, see my vision tunneling in from the edges.

And that's when Cedric, beautiful unshaven Cedric, glorious lord of the aerosol can, busts out of the bathroom door with his pants around his ankles and his withered old penis flopping around. He's screaming at the top of his lungs and waving his hands. *"I crapped my pants,"* he shrieks. Then his ankles tangle up in his smeared underwear and he goes down with a crash, taking the snack cakes shelf with him in a tremendous crash.

I find myself able to move again. The store quiet except for Cedric's moaning. When I turn my head back, the little man and his suitcase are gone. Nothing but a couple of slow old houseflies bumbling against the plate-glass windows. Cedric's moaning and mumbling to himself on the floor, and he sure smells like he messed himself. I swallow; no motion, no twitching lump. My fly is quiet again, back in whatever metaphysical innards it usually hides in.

The store is empty.

And of course I'm the one who has to scrub Cedric's stains off the floor and wipe down the snack cakes–you'd better believe I put 'em back on the shelf; that shit comes out of my pay if I have to trash it. I even do a couple of the Phantom's cleaning assignments. Kind of a lot of nervous energy to work off, you know?

I've never seen the little man and his buzzing suitcase again. I kind of wonder sometimes. When you make a deal with the devil, you're supposed to get something real nice out of it, aren't you? Money, power, fame. Meantime I'm sitting here eating Top Ramen and Kraft Macaroni and

Cheese every night, working the worst shift in the worst job in the world and having to feel grateful to get even that, and all the while my loan debt plays the boulder to my Sisyphus, and I think to myself, how badly do I need that thing inside me, really? What has it ever done for me? Maybe it's not so bad in that suitcase.

At least I'd have lots of friends.

GREEKS BEARING GIFTS

ILENE GOLDMAN

J.D. punched the numbers again and threw the calculator against the wall. It hit the worn linoleum with a clatter. Eighteen months of unemployment benefits, gone. A lifetime of savings, run out. J.D. had just enough to cover next month's rent—if he didn't eat, use the phone, or turn on a light. Not where he'd planned to be after twenty-three years at the plant.

He stared at the calendar. Tomorrow was payday. A whole $83 after taxes for the one day of temp work he'd gotten in the last two weeks, only the second day of work he'd had in three months. The temp agency did its best to rotate its long list of men through its small list of jobs, but it was never enough.

And how much of that $83 would J.D. actually see? The court was garnishing his meager wages for back alimony and child support—which he'd gladly pay if he had the funds. Not for the first time, J.D. wondered if everyone would be better off with him dead.

Maybe he could sell a few more of his sparse furnishings. The kitchen table and chairs could go. He ate most of his meals in his armchair. The laptop could go. It wasn't much use without the internet, and he'd given up that subscription six months ago. He could do without the microwave, too. How much would all that fetch?

A knock on the door stopped him cold. Damn collection agents. Those vultures could pry his last pennies from his cold, dead hands.

Another knock.

J.D. bit his tongue. Yelling at the bastards would only encourage them. Better to ignore them. They'd go away eventually.

One more knock and then the swish of something sliding under the door.

J.D. waited until the footsteps faded before investigating. A business card. That was new.

Morton Décès
FINAL SOLUTION FINANCIAL SERVICES
We make your money problems go away.

"Yeah, right." J.D. flipped the card into the trash. Even as a kid, he hadn't believed in fairy tales.

———

THE NEXT DAY, as J.D. scrubbed the last of the tomato sauce stains from the microwave, he heard another knock on the door. The same crisp knock, the same rhythm, as the day before.

J.D.'s eyes focused on the envelopes stacked on his counter, every one with a blood-red FINAL NOTICE or PAST DUE stamp. The stack had grown by three with today's mail delivery. It would only get bigger tomorrow.

Maybe he should hear what these financial services people had to say. It didn't cost anything to listen.

J.D. opened the door after the second knock.

The man in the hall was tall, thin, and angular. He wore a dark suit, crisp white shirt, and perfectly symmetrical red tie. One of his bony hands held a shiny black briefcase. He held out the other. "Sir, I'm Morton Décès from Final Solutions Financial Services. How are you today?"

"Fine." J.D. shook the man's hand, trying not to wince at the cold clamminess.

"May I come in?"

J.D. glanced over his shoulder.

"This won't take long." Décès leaned in and dropped his voice to a hiss-like whisper. "I find money matters are best discussed in private."

J.D. stepped back so the man could pass.

Décès settled himself at the table, his briefcase opening with a snap. Taking out a legal pad and pen, he slid the case to the side and gestured at the opposite seat. "Please."

J.D. slid into the chair, suddenly a stranger in his own apartment.

Décès poised his pen above the pad. "Tell me about your finances."

J.D.'s gut tied itself into a knot. Give his financial information to a complete stranger? He was desperate, not stupid. "Before we get to that, I have a few questions."

Décès set down his pen and quickly clenched and then unclenched his fists. "Of course."

J.D. leaned forward. "How did you get my name?"

"I didn't. You haven't shared it with me yet."

"You knocked on my door by chance?"

"I wouldn't say *chance*. I'm a door-to-door salesman. I knock on many doors."

"You sell financial planning door to door?" J.D.'s eyebrows almost reached his hairline.

"Not financial planning, no. That requires money. We assist individuals on the other end of the financial spectrum."

"But door to door?"

There was something practiced about the way Décès shrugged. "What can I say? I'm an old-fashioned man doing an old-fashioned job."

J.D. let that sit. "And what financial services does your firm offer?"

Décès pulled a shiny brochure out of his briefcase and slid it across the table. J.D. kept his focus on Décès's face.

"We provide a wide variety of services, which allows us to cater to each client's individual needs."

"And your rates?"

"Competitive." Décès must have seen J.D.'s face fall. "But flexible."

"Define *flexible*."

Décès leaned back in his chair and tented his long fingers. "We have occasionally had a client... fall short. For them, we have restructured their payment plans, or accepted payment of a... different kind."

J.D. turned that over a few times. "Do you ever repossess or use collection agencies?"

"In extreme cases, yes, unfortunately, we have. But those cases have been few and far between. We try to work with our clients to avoid such... unhappy endings."

"So what can you do for me?"

Décès grinned. It wasn't pretty. There was something off about it, like the grin was too big for his face. It reminded J.D. of the Cheshire cat. That damn thing had given him nightmares for months as a child.

Décès picked up his pen. "Why don't we start with your name?"

"Jason Donovan, but everyone calls me J.D."

Décès scribbled on his pad. "And, Mr. Donovan, what would you say is your most immediate financial need?"

"Getting my life back."

The financial planner raised an eyebrow, Spock-style, so J.D. explained his situation. As he talked, his hands shook.

Décès put his hand on J.D.'s. It felt chilly, like he'd been holding an ice pack. "Mr. Donovan, I assure you, yours is not the first tale of woe I have heard. Hardship is no stranger around here."

That was true. The town had been dying since the plant closed. Those who could move away, had. Everyone else, J.D. included, struggled to make ends meet.

Décès pulled his hand back, flipped to a new page of his pad, and scribbled quickly. Turning the page to face J.D., he said, "This is what I can do for you."

He walked J.D. through his plan, item by item. By the time he left, the sun had set, a full moon was rising, and J.D. had signed on the dotted line.

————

WHEN THE PHONE jangled the next morning, J.D. answered without thinking. Only after he'd lifted the receiver did it occur to him that it might be a collection agency.

"J.D.?" His ex sounded tinny and, surprisingly, not angry.

"Joannie?"

"I just wanted to say thank you."

J.D.'s thoughts raced. What had he done?

"The check was delivered today. You didn't have to pay everything all at once, and you certainly didn't have to include the extra."

"Yeah, well…"

"I just wanted you to know that me and Nick, we appreciate it."

She hung up before J.D. could say anything more. Not that he had anything to add. His brain was still trying to catch up.

Décès! He'd said the first step was settling J.D.'s debts. But that was *last night*. How had he managed to take care of everything so quickly?

J.D. shook his head. *Don't look a gift horse in the mouth, man.*

———

WITH JOANNIE off his back and the collection agencies silenced, J.D. found some breathing room. He traded his dollar ramen dinners for boxed mac and cheese. He stepped lighter, and he even found himself smiling at passersby. And finally, finally, he was getting some nibbles on his job applications. To celebrate, J.D. allowed himself a beer at the local bar.

He wandered home under the light of the full moon. He fumbled with the key but finally managed to get the door open. He groped for the switch. The light revealed Décès sitting at the table.

The tall man looked eerie, sharper and more angular than usual and ghostly pale. "Mr. Donovan, I am so glad you're home. We have business to discuss."

J.D. blinked. "Now? How'd you get in?"

"Your landlord was most helpful, and yes, I'm afraid we have to do this now."

J.D. flopped into a chair. He tried to focus, but the beer and the late hour made it difficult.

"As you know, Mr. Donovan, we advanced quite a bit of money on your account."

"Yes. Thank you. I can't tell you how much—"

Décès brushed away J.D.'s words. "It's time to make a payment, Mr. Donovan."

"A payment? I never received a statement."

"We don't use statements." Décès leaned forward. "We take care of such business in person. That's what allows us to be flexible."

"But I haven't found work yet."

"Then perhaps you can name a proxy. Someone to stand up for you."

J.D. didn't hesitate. Only one person still had his back: Gallagher, his old foreman at the plant.

Décès wrote down the name. "Thank you, Mr. Donovan. I will see you again."

———

GALLAGHER'S DEATH was front page in the morning paper.

J.D. barely made it to the bathroom before his breakfast came back up.

J.D. wiped his mouth, rinsed the sink, and took a few calming breaths before returning to the table.

The article was more eulogy than news report. It named Gallagher's family—a daughter, a son, three grandchildren, and a wife of thirty years—and described his involvement in the community: the Lions Club, Boy Scouts, Little League, and VFW.

None of it told J.D. what he wanted to know: had Gallagher saved his old employee's ass before he died?

———

THE NEXT MONTH, J.D. was ready. He'd scrounged some day labor and wrangled a couple days of temp work. The cash sat in an envelope on the table.

Décès laughed as he pocketed the money. "My dear Mr. Donovan. I applaud the effort, but this is not nearly enough."

"How much more do you need?"

Décès shrugged. "Another name. Perhaps another coworker?"

J.D. turned cold. "You saw Gallagher?"

"I did, indeed." Décès nodded, his expression stony and bland. "His passing was most unfortunate. You have my condolences."

"Thank you." Décès's words sounded more formal than heartfelt to J.D., but what had he expected?

The two men sat in silence, the air heavy with expectation. J.D. traced the grain of the table top. Another coworker? He could count on one hand the ones who were left. They were not his favorite people, and he hadn't been one of theirs.

Décès watched, a hawk studying its prey. Finally, he tapped his watch. "Mr. Donovan, I'm afraid I need a name."

J.D. shook his head. "I can't."

"Now, Mr. Donovan."

J.D. huffed. After a moment of thought, he named the best of the worst. "Charlie. Charlie Simmons."

"Thank you." Décès swept the envelope off the table and disappeared out the door.

J.D. wanted to sigh with relief, but the butterflies dancing in his insides wouldn't let him.

———

J.D. WALKED on tenterhooks for days. By Friday night, he couldn't take it anymore. He grabbed a tenner from the month's money envelope and headed for the bar. The least he could do was warn Charlie.

But Charlie wasn't there. Not at the pool table he usually hustled. Not at the corner table he usually occupied. Not at any seat at the bar. Not even in the dingy men's room in the back.

J.D. searched the room for a familiar face, someone who might know where Charlie was, but came up empty. He hoisted himself onto a stool at the bar.

He ordered a cheap beer and asked, "Hey, you wouldn't have seen Charlie Simmons around lately, have ya?"

The bartender shook her head. "Haven't seen him all week."

J.D. frowned. "Thanks."

The bar door swung open and banged shut. The bartender nodded at the newcomer. "Ask Gray. He might know."

"Might know what?" Gray sidled up next to J.D. From the smell of him, he'd already gotten a few under his belt.

"Where Charlie's been." The bartender put a little flirt in her voice. "It's not like him to leave me alone so long."

Gray grinned. "Guess you'll have to settle for me, then." The grin vanished, and a pall fell over him. "Charlie's in the hospital. Been there since Tuesday? Wednesday? Something like that."

A chill went down J.D.'s spine. "The hospital? Anything serious?"

The bartender slid a shot in front of Gray. He picked it up and downed it in a single move. "I'll say. Docs can't figure out what's wrong. They've been running tests and doing scans, and they all say everything's normal. Even though Charlie ain't."

Gray downed another shot. "They're talking about exploratory surgery, cutting him from stem to stern and poking around to see what they can find."

"Jesus." The bartender looked as pale as J.D. felt.

J.D. tightened his grip on his beer. "What happened? He seemed fine last Friday."

"Sure did." Gray nodded. "Kicked my ass at the pool table, like always. A few days later, completely out of the blue, he started wheezing. A few minutes after that, he clutched his chest and collapsed. Been in and out of consciousness ever since. Cora's beside herself." Gray called for another shot.

J.D. laid his hand on Gray's shoulder. "Charlie's a tough SOB. If anyone can pull through, he can. Let Cora know I'll be praying for them both."

He trembled all the way home.

———

J.D. RETURNED to the bar the next night and the night after that and the night after that, desperate for news of Charlie. He became more regular than the regulars. He always sat at the bar, but never on the same stool twice in a row and always nursing one cheap beer each night. He learned the bartender was named Lisa, her father had worked at the plant until he retired and moved to Arizona, and, she—like so many others in town—was saving up to get out. Thankfully for her, bars were the one industry in town that was still thriving.

Pool table gossip kept J.D. informed of Charlie's condition. If anything, he'd gotten worse. Doctors referred to his condition as a coma but remained baffled by the specifics.

Charlie passed at the end of the month, his diagnosis still a mystery. Lisa broke the news before J.D. grabbed his stool. He skipped his usual beer that night in favor of a shot of Charlie's favorite whiskey.

Lisa joined him. "To Charlie."

They clinked glasses and threw back the firewater.

"Funeral's Thursday," Lisa said. "Everyone will be gathering here after."

J.D. made a vow to go.

———

THE BAR WAS PACKED the night of the funeral, and every person had a Charlie story. Most were about pool hustles or drunken escapades, but a few were about the favor of a loyal friend. J.D. kept his story to himself, seated at the end of the bar nursing his usual beer.

Someone sidled up on J.D.'s left. A chill washed over him.

"Mr. Donovan, did you forget our appointment?" Décès could not have sounded more condescending if he tried.

J.D. didn't look up from his drink. "Afraid so."

Décès placed a cold hand on J.D.'s elbow. "Then why don't we retire to your abode so we can take care of business?"

J.D. yanked his arm away. "No. I'm staying here. I'm mourning a friend. You'll get your money but not tonight."

"Ah, but I'm afraid it must be tonight. Those are the terms of our agreement."

J.D. took a swig of beer. "What happened to all that flexibility you promised? Does it really make all that much difference if you get your money at 9:00 A.M. instead of 9:00 P.M.?"

"As a matter of fact, it does." Décès grabbed J.D.'s beer with two fingers and placed it out of J.D.'s reach. He gestured toward the door. "Shall we?"

As J.D. rose to reach for his drink, Lisa the Bartender slid to their end of the bar. She placed her hands on her hips. "Is there a problem here?"

Décès dropped his hand and bowed his head. "No, ma'am. Not at all."

"That's not quite true." J.D. grabbed his beer and fell back onto his seat. "I owe Mr. Décès some money, and he's insisting I get it for him right this very minute."

Lisa shrugged. "Surely a few dollars can wait until morning. This is a wake, after all."

J.D. turned toward Décès and raised his eyebrows.

Décès's cordiality became condescension. "I'm afraid, young lady, the arrangement is not as informal as Mr. Donovan implies."

Lisa narrowed her eyes and crossed her arms, her hands folded into fists. Her clenched jaw twitched. Not even rude, handsy customers earned that level of ire. "Frankly, sir, I don't give a damn about your 'arrangement.' I do give a damn about my boys, one of whom is being mourned here tonight. Now, if J.D. says he's good for it, he's good for it, and you'd do well to take him at his word. You'll get your damn money tomorrow."

J.D. bit his cheek, keeping his eyes on Décès.

Décès stared at Lisa, his features sharper and colder than J.D. had ever seen them. Lisa stared right back.

Décès leaned forward, his hand sliding across the bar toward the bartender. "Ma'am, is my understanding correct? Are you vouching for Mr. Donovan here?"

Lisa leaned back on her heels. "I am."

Décès slapped the bar and nodded. "Very well." He held out his hand to J.D. "Until next time, then, Mr. Donovan."

J.D. nodded in return, then downed the rest of his beer, the bottle landing on the bar with a loud clunk. He chugged two more beers in quick succession, but neither quieted the churning in his stomach.

———

THE NEXT MORNING, J.D. woke late and hungover, guilt gnawing at his gut. What the hell had he done? He stumbled into the bathroom, threw cold water on his face, and tossed back some ibuprofen. Wet but no more awake, he made his way to the kitchen and his coffee machine. Thank God he hadn't sold that. Cup of joe in hand, he flopped into his chair and wracked his sore head, pulling his memory reluctantly through the events of the previous day.

By the time he got to Charlie's wake, the painkiller was kicking in and his mind was starting to clear.

Décès. He'd been there, at the bar.

And Lisa...

J.D. dropped his cup. Was she okay?

He couldn't wait to find out. The bar opened at noon. It was after 11:00 now. He stuffed ten dollars in his pocket and headed out, spilled coffee be damned.

————

Roy, the bar's owner, found J.D. sitting on the front stoop when he opened the front door.

"Donovan, you're here early."

J.D. jumped to his feet. "I'm looking for Lisa. What time does she get in?"

Roy frowned and shook his head. "She's not. She called in sick."

J.D.'s mouth went dry. Hungover like him sick, or dying like Charlie sick? He slid onto a stool and tapped the bar for a drink.

"Never took you for a day drinker." Roy grabbed a bottle of J.D.'s usual and pushed it across the bar.

"Hair of the dog, my friend." J.D. held the bottle in a toast before taking a swig. Bottle back on the bar, he fiddled with the label. "So Lisa, is she...?"

Roy snorted. "You two start dating and not tell anyone?"

"No, it's not that. It's just... something happened last

night, and I want to make sure she's okay. That's all."

Instantly, Roy was all business—straight posture, straighter expression. "What happened?"

J.D. hesitated.

Roy put both hands on the bar. "I don't tolerate any shit in my bar. What the hell happened, Donovan?"

J.D. took a deep breath and gave Roy the short version of Décès's visit. "Boundaries are not something this guy seems to understand. I just want to make sure he didn't hassle Lisa after I left."

Roy nodded. He pulled his cellphone from his shirt pocket and dialed. Handing the phone to J.D., he said, "Ask her yourself."

Six rings later, Lisa's voicemail picked up. J.D. tried to sound casual. "Hey, Lisa. J.D. from the bar. Just wanted to make sure you got home okay. Give Roy a call when you can. Thanks."

He handed the phone back to Roy, thanked him, and trudged back home. He took the long way, hoping to settle his uneasiness. By the time he reached his door, he knew the only way to ease his nerves was to see Lisa for himself.

He went to grab his laptop. Damn it. He didn't have any internet, did he?

J.D. checked his phone and found he'd reached the limit of his plan for that month. Time for Option C.

He dug his bus pass out of the drawer and headed for the library. Twenty-five minutes and one Google search later, he had Lisa's address. Two bus transfers and a short walk after that, he was at Lisa's front door.

He knocked.

No answer.

He punched the doorbell.

No answer.

He knocked again, this time calling Lisa's name.

No answer.

He leaned over to peer through the window. The crack in the blinds didn't give him a wide view, but it was enough to tell the lights were out and the TV was off. There was no movement, no signs of life.

J.D. felt eyes on his back. He turned. A curtain fluttered in the neighbor's window.

He jogged over and knocked on the door. It opened as far as the chain lock would allow.

"I'm sorry to bother you." J.D. waved toward Lisa's house. "I'm a friend of Lisa's. We were at a wake last night and celebrated a little too much, if you know what I mean. I wanted to make sure she got home okay. Have you seen her?"

The gray eye that peered through the cracked door gave him a once-over.

"Please? I tried calling but she didn't answer. She's not answering the door, either. That's not like her."

Another once-over. A grimace. Then, in a rough voice that could only be the result of decades of smoking, "Yeah, I saw her."

J.D. sighed, his whole body sagging with relief.

"But you're not going to like it."

J.D. snapped to. "What do you mean?"

"There was a man waiting for her when she got home. Tall, narrow drink of water. They had a few words, and she went off with him, his hand on her back. She ain't been home since."

Tall, narrow drink of water. That could only be Décès. J.D. muttered thanks and backed away from the door. On his three-bus ride home, the pieces slid into place.

A week later, his suspicions were confirmed.

Lisa's body was found in an abandoned house.

———

J.D. WANTED to be ready when the next full moon came. By now, he knew Décès didn't want money. He wanted names. Lives. But how to stop Décès? Would he accept J.D.'s name? Was J.D. willing to make that sacrifice? By month's end, J.D. had the makings of an ulcer, but no answer.

Décès's crisp knock came right on time. The man was nothing if not efficient.

J.D. took a deep breath and smoothed his hair. He wiped his hands on his pants and then opened the door. He waved Décès inside.

Décès wore the same suit, carried the same briefcase, as when J.D. first met him. As a matter of fact, he'd been wearing that suit every time J.D. saw him. That had to mean something, but what?

Décès held out his hand. "Your payment, Mr. Donovan?"

J.D. straightened. "I don't have it."

"Then I'll need a name."

J.D. shook his head. "Nope."

"Mr. Donovan, you know how this works. You either pay me in full, or give me the name of someone who can vouch for you."

"Vouch for me? What does that mean exactly? Do they sign a piece of paper? Give you money? Because as far as I can tell, vouching for me means they die, and that is not a fair trade." J.D. balled his hands into fists and jammed them into his pockets.

Décès's smile was icy. "As I'm sure your own experience has taught you, Mr. Donovan, life is not fair. You signed a contract, and those were its terms. Now, who will it be?"

"I'm not giving you another name."

"Your son, Nick, perhaps? Or maybe his mother?"

J.D. exploded. "You bastard! What gives you the right to threaten my son's life?"

"I'm simply listing your options. Each of your friends

bought you one month and one month only."

What would happen if he refused? Would Décès take his life, even though he hadn't offered it? What choice did he have? J.D. hadn't been a very good father and he'd been an even worse husband, but Joannie and Nick shouldn't pay for his mistakes. If it came down to Nick's life or his own, there was no contest.

J.D. breathed deeply, searching for an escape route. An idea took shape. He met Décès's gaze. "I'm ready."

Décès raised his eyebrow. "And?"

"How does it work?"

"You give me the name. Same as before."

"No." J.D. planted his feet and crossed his arms. "If I'm going to be responsible for taking a life, then I want—I need —to actually do the deed."

"If you insist." Décès produced a thick black candle, a fire-place match, and a card. He pushed them across the table. "You light the candle with that match. You read the words on the card, then you say the name."

Not the answer J.D. had expected, but far easier than he'd imagined. He struck the match and touched it to the candle's wick. Once the flame caught, J.D. sounded out the words on the card. Then he slowly pronounced the name, "Morton Décès."

Décès smiled his Cheshire cat grin. He clapped his hands. "Bravo! I'm afraid, though, that's not how it—"

Décès blinked. He seemed pinched. He struggled for breath and grabbed his middle. He bent in half, gasping for air. His body trembled and convulsed. In the blink of an eye and a puff of smoke, Décès was gone.

J.D. stared at the empty chair. It took a few seconds for him to remember to breathe. He blew out the candle and collapsed into the nearest seat. "It seems, Mr. Décès, that's exactly how it works."

SWEET MEATS: A GRISLY TALE
OF HANSEL AND GRETEL
TIM KANE

F rom my perch high on a branch, its bark scratchy and
infested with lichen, I watched two children meander
between the trees, tossing chunks of bloody meat onto the
snow-laden forest floor.

A sputter of half-frozen slush dribbled from above,
squarely onto my head. I flapped what I thought of as arms,
though now transformed into raven's wings, and shook my
feathers dry.

The villagers never braved the woods unless it was to
seek out my skills as a healer and a witch. Yet these children
seemed to wander with no set purpose. And I could not
recall their names. Although I rarely visited the hamlet at the
edge of these woods, the settlement was a small one, where
only rumor and gossip shifted with the seasons. Seldom the
faces. These two were new additions.

The girl wore her blonde hair in plaits, hanging along her
back like twin yellow ropes. She had on a green dress, its
long hem skimming the snow. The boy, plumper than his
companion, dressed only in pants, a shirt, and simple leather

shoes. How did the pair not freeze? Even their hands were gloveless, fingers stained red with the blood of their meaty scraps.

What concern were they to me? The two journeyed not in the direction of my home. Perhaps it was some macabre amusement devised by the villagers to brighten up their winter days. I spread my wings and received another drizzle of frigid water for my efforts.

A scream broke the silence. The sound of an animal in suffering.

Scanning the woods, I spied figures farther off. More villagers? Leaping off the branch, my wings bit the icy air. The girl caught my movement and followed me with her gaze, the curl of a smirk forming on her lips.

Up ahead... it had to be nearly the whole hamlet, the villager's clothes soiled nearly black. What had happened? I knew these people, simple farmers, all of them. Now transformed into ravenous beasts.

A group swarmed a fallen stag, tearing the animal apart. The remainder surrounded a doe and her fawn, tightening the circle. The doe let out a series of panicked grunts as it turned about, trying to stay in front of her child.

The villagers stared at the deer, bits of gore dangling from their mouths—from the stag or the scraps the children had discarded? I could not tell.

The ring of villagers constricted. Their teeth clacked together in imagined biting. One swiped at the doe, leaving a spattered handprint on her flank.

Enough.

I swooped down and my talons struck their mark. Claws sunk into the attacker's eyes. He wailed in surprise and fell backward into the snow, dragging me down with him. With the circle broken, the doe and fawn leapt through the opening, their hooves cutting the air above my head.

As I raised my wings, making ready to fly, a hand seized one wingtip. The eyeless villager, groping about in blackness, found me. I flapped my other wing and hopped onto the snowy ground. Yet still he clung. The others crowded around, drawn by my frantic movements. Hands descended, from every side. I tore my wing free, leaving three black feathers in the eyeless man's grip.

The villagers clutched for me, but I swept past them to the sky. Circling high, I wanted to put plenty of distance between myself and this horde. The doe and fawn had escaped, but no such luck for the stag.

From the air I spotted a trail of carcasses snaking toward the hamlet. Every animal the villagers encountered met the same fate as the stag. Only the swift or the lucky escaped. And still the children scattered their bloody morsels, leading the villagers deeper into the woods.

Back at my cottage, I glided through the windowsill. My wounded wing throbbed. Each movement speckled the dirt floor with blood. I sucked in a deep breath and felt my bones lengthen—the anguish of stretched muscle and sinew. Gradually, feathers sloughed off as my limbs elongated. Human feet replaced talons, wings shifted into arms. Why was transforming back always more arduous than becoming a bird? Some cruel twist inflicted by magic. I detested the whole process.

Yet how I adored to fly.

I lay on the floor of my cottage, panting, skin slick with sweat. After nearly sixty years on this earth, my body had become a collection of creaking bones and aching muscles. Ah, to be young and witless again.

I rose and draped a cloak about my naked form. When I flexed my left hand, the fingertips stung. Blood collected where the nails should be. Three missing in all, corresponding to the feathers the villager had torn free. The wound carried over into my human form.

Even bandaged, my fingers still bled. I recalled the fallen stag. How the villagers mobbed it, tearing the animal apart, bits of flesh hanging from their lips. They would not stop at just the one animal. It was not in their nature. People always sought more and soon their hunger would devour the whole woods.

The solution lay with the girl and the boy, who could only be malignant spirits masquerading as children. I must cut the head off the snake. Dispose of the children who had corrupted the villagers with their foul sorcery.

Out my window, brittle branches jutted up and cast long shadows across the snow. I had flown nearly a mile. Yet the children led the villagers westward, toward the setting sun. A course parallel to my cottage.

If cankerous spirits these children were, then only fire could burn the evil away. I pushed a heap of newly fallen snow from my windowsill. Wet wood cannot be set alight. Only my own hearth could burn hot enough.

So I must lure them here.

I went to work quickly, consulting my books and gathering ingredients. I swung the iron pot over the fire and lived it up with dry logs. I needed the flames to blaze with hellish heat. My hearth was wide and deep, large enough to spit a deer. But I had lost the taste for meat long ago, after learning the spell of transforming. Hard to eat the flesh of an animal when you become one yourself.

All the while I glanced out the window and was rewarded with a view of the woods. No sign of the children or their horde of villagers. Each passing moment they traveled farther away. Soon, they would be beyond my power.

With the concoction finished, I hauled the pot outside. Using a brush, I slathered the mixture on the cottage stones.

Even after the first stroke, the product of my magic filled the air with the stink of decaying meat. Yet there was also a sugary sweetness to it. As the fading sunlight glinted off the wet stones, the concoction shimmered. Illusion took hold of the cottage. The stacked stone walls became piles of festering meat. The straw roof transmuted into dripping offal. Even my front door changed, from stout oak boards to a collection of stitched-together bones, each with a skin of gristle.

A little of the concoction remained. This I sealed in the pot and hauled inside. With the trap set, now I waited, letting the scent of meat lure the villagers. Would my magic be greater than the children's? For the sake of the woods, I hoped so.

It did not take long. The two children appeared at the edge of the clearing. As they approached, my suspicions were confirmed. A tail of matted hair dangled from beneath the girl's skirt, dragging along the snow. The boy showed no outward sign of the demonic, though his shoes might well hide cloven feet. The list of demons ran long, but I suspected these two were imps masquerading as children. Yes, easy enough to handle. Yet uncertainty gnawed at my mind. Cacodaemons often took human form. And far more dreadful these creatures were.

All the while, the children's unblinking gaze settled on my cottage—now rebuilt into a carnivore's feast.

I pushed my shutters nearly closed, allowing only a crack to peek through. The pocket of my apron held several iron nails and I clutched a small hammer. The best defense against magical creatures.

When they arrived at my doorstep, the boy reached toward the meat walls glistening in the evening light, his fingers still bloody from his own scraps. The girl slapped his hand.

"It is but an illusion. Witch magic." The girl surveyed the cottage. "Come out, Rosina. We want to see your face."

Doubt needled my skin. So they knew me. Perhaps these two were stronger than I could cope with. Still, I could not delay the inevitable. I pulled the door open, careful to keep the hammer behind my back.

The girl sauntered through, her manner relaxed as though nothing in this world could harm her. The tail peeked from beneath her skirts, swishing this way and that. As she moved, I noted her footsteps on my dusty earthen floor, each one clear and precise, and gripped the hammer tightly. Then the boy blundered in, shuffling his shoes and obliterating any sign of the girl's passage.

"We shall devour these woods," the girl announced. "And you along with them." She grinned, displaying teeth pointed like needles.

The fire cast her in an orange glow. The boy trundled toward the shadowy perimeter of my cottage, knocking over my spinning wheel and a ceramic jug of vinegar.

I cleared my throat. "I am but a feeble woman with nothing you need."

"You lie." The girl clicked her nails against my vials, leaving smears from her bloody fingers. "Your worthless magic will not protect you. Not from us."

"Who are you?"

The boy stepped into the firelight and thumped his chest. "We are the mighty caco…"

The girl slapped him across the face. He gave her an icy look but slunk away.

A shiver ran through me. Cacodaemons. Tenacious creatures. Once one gained a foothold in our world; the thing was nearly impossible to extricate. Here I had a pair of them.

"We are the fire sent to cleanse this world." A grin appeared on the girl's lips again.

I glanced down. The boy's muddy tracks littered the doorway, easy to catch. But I needed a clear imprint from the girl.

A rabble of voices drifted from outside. Through the window, I spied the horde of villagers tromping out of the woods. Once in the clearing, the sight of the transformed cottage acted like a beacon and they scrambled over each other to reach it.

Absentmindedly, my hand dipped into the apron pocket, fingering the nails. The iron prickled my skin, dampening any magic it touched. When I looked up, the girl wore another one of those smirks. She ran a finger along the leather-bound books set upon my mantle, the flames below casting all in an orange hue.

I gripped a nail in one hand, readying the hammer in the other.

The girl flicked her tail, causing the skirt to billow. Then she stepped away, leaving a clear imprint in the ashes by the hearth.

Now was the time.

I knelt and jammed a nail into the muddy footprint of the boy. The instant my hammer struck the iron head, he shrieked in agony. Although he stood several feet away, blood leaked from the seams of his shoe and his foot became rooted to the spot—held there by the magic of the iron nail.

But where was the girl? She'd vanished. Firelight flickered, causing shadows to jitter across the contents of my cottage. Could she have changed shape? Twisted her body into some smaller form?

I edged closer to the hearth and the imprint of her foot in the ashes. Each flutter of the shadows might be the girl. There, a gleam of light. But only a glass jug. And there, something shifted along the ground. But it was just the fluctuation of the firelight. Through it all, the boy howled, yanking up at his leg.

I had reached the hearth and the outline of the girl's slender foot. My hand fumbled in the apron pocket for another nail. I flicked my gaze around the cottage. Was that a shape behind the boy, huddled in the dark?

Quick, while I held the advantage, I glanced down and placed the nail on the footprint. A cackle of laughter joined the boy's cries. The girl lunged from the shadows, hands outstretched.

I raised the hammer. But she moved with inhuman speed and shoved me into the fire.

Dropping the hammer, I gripped her arm, dragging her in with me. Flames swirled up, the heat blasting everything. Smoke choked the air. Instantly my eyes watered. Breathing fragmented into gagging. The fire set alight my robe—flames crackling through the fabric and scalding my flesh.

The girl only giggled.

I summoned the last of my magic and wrenched my bones inward. Muscles crushed together, crammed into a smaller form. Feathers jutted out — a thousand needles punching through my skin. My robes fell away, momentarily dampening the heat of the flames. I leapt into the air, wings already smoldering, and shot up the chimney.

I managed to reach clear night air before sputtering onto the thatched roof. I rested on packed straw, sucking in breath after breath. The edges of the roof glistened with blood, that being as far as I could reach with the smeared concoction.

The horde of villagers descended upon my cottage, like ants swarming over a dribble of honey. Hands reached up. Each time they snatched a handful of bloody offal, the glamour broke, leaving only a clump of straw. Yet they did not stop.

I hopped to the edge, saw their bodies pressing forward.

Always the click, click, click of their teeth. Most could not reach and so chewed empty air. But those closer crunched down on stone and straw. Bit by bit, they tore apart my cottage.

"Rosina!" It was the girl, laughter filling her voice.

How could that be? I'd pulled her into the flames.

I scurried across the roof to a spot bare of thatching and peered into the cottage. The girl stood in the center of the room, skin scorched raw by the flames, hair half burned away. Her clothes turned to ash. Yet she grinned, needle teeth protruding now, like tiny tusks. Her tail whisked back and forth, smoke curling from the charred hair.

Her skin grew pale and the scalded flesh vanished, as though it were nothing but a wisp of mist. Even the blonde hair regrew, regaining its luster, the strands intertwining into plaits once more. Save for her naked form, she was whole again, as though the flames had never touched her.

The girl snatched a thin branch from the fire and scampered to the front door. I pressed my raven's head close to watch. There she knelt and with the branch knocked the nail from the floor. The boy stumbled, finally able to move. At first he favored the uninjured foot. But after a moment, he too must have healed because he strutted around the cottage, pulling down shelves and tossing books into the fire.

"You see! Nothing can hurt us." The girl shouted at the whole cottage. Perhaps even the entire world. "All is ours."

I abandoned my home, flying deeper into the woods. All the while, the sounds of the villagers' chomping filled my mind. They would demolish my cottage. What next? How far could I hope to go? Nothing would quench the tide of their insatiable hunger.

I came across a cluster of stones with a hollow free of snow. There I landed. In the distance, flames sparkled in the night air. They had set the roof ablaze. By now the cottage would be reduced to rubble. I huddled in a crevice between the mossen rocks, pulling my wings close against my body.

Many hours later, the sun's rays sliced through the trees. Melting snow trickled along my back. I wriggled free from my stony hollow. Only a thin smear of smoke signaled the location of the cottage. My home, gone.

Neither animal nor bird stirred. The woods were quiet. Had the horde departed? Led onward by those wicked hell-children? Despite how agreeable this notion appeared, it felt false in my heart.

Raising my wings, I shook away the dampness. The girl had been right. This was all too much for my meager skills. I could outfly their voracious hunger. Let them have these woods.

I turned away from the cottage, ready to soar into the sky. But there stood the doe, her fawn cowering a few paces behind. Both looked down at me, their dark eyes like wet river pebbles. I held their gaze, willing them to glance away. But they would not.

This was their home, too. The bloody cravings of the villagers would not end here. The demon-spell would spread, infecting hamlet after hamlet. How far could I really fly? To the ends of the world?

No. I would not abandon my home.

I took to the air, circling higher until the doe was but a speck against the white blanket of winter. The tendril of black smoke slithered above the woods. As I glided over the trees, the air grew polluted—the scent of charred wood mixed with the foul reek of spoiled meat.

I located my little clearing, now bare earth scorched black with fire. Larger stones lay in scattered heaps, the remnants of the cottage walls. And all around, the slumbering bodies of the villagers, strewn upon each other like tumbled sticks. The two children curled in the ashes of my hearth, as though the glowing embers served as a blanket. The girl still stark naked, her clothes the only part of her affected by the fire.

I landed a good distance away and approached, wary should the villagers rise up. Yet none did. All of them sluggish, their bellies full—packed no doubt with the smaller rocks from the cottage walls. A precious few of my possessions survived, and only those objects that proved inedible. Fireplace tongs lay bent and twisted. A horn, collected from a dying ram, poked out from beneath a slumbering villager, its surface marred from gnawing. And my black iron cauldron. It had the good fortune of being submerged by a collapsing wall. Stones piled up around it like a tiny hillock.

Could it still be intact? I dared not hope lest some twist of fate make it not so.

I began the transformation, muscles pulled taut, bones jerking outward. This time the change did not come all at once, as though my body, weary of the hardships already endured, would not budge from raven's form. I panted and gasped, driving my arms outward. When at long last, I thrust myself back into human form, I lay there, on the dirt, sweat streaking my bare body. Despite the chill in the morning air, my skin burned feverously. It would be some time before I could transform again.

A blanket, torn and chewed but still whole, lay in the dirt beside me. This became my meager clothes. I attempted to stand, but my legs tottered and sent me back to the ground. On hands and knees then, on toward the cauldron. Gripping one of the stones, I heaved it aside. Several more cascaded down, creating a racket of collisions. My blood froze. This would wake the horde for sure. I glanced at the slumbering bodies around me. The villagers stirred but did not wake. A jittery relief swept over me.

Taking care to be as quiet as possible, I removed the remaining stones from the cauldron. It was intact, not a single crack marred its surface. The leftovers of my concoction, still safe inside.

Grabbing the handle, I hauled the cauldron toward the hearth and the two dozing children. The fire had already taught me their indifference to harm. Any injury they sustained would heal again.

I slid the lid off the cauldron. The sickly sweet smell of meat rose into the air. Already, I sensed the villagers tremble, woken by their insatiable hunger. I worked with haste, using the brush left inside. I slathered the concoction across the boy first, knowing he would be least likely to wake. Within moments, the sticky residue covered his clothes. He remained asleep, his breathing steady.

The villagers rose up, sedate in their motions. Yet I detected an eagerness in their eyes. In moments, they would surge forward.

I turned to the girl, her nude form curled on the ashes, tail tucked between her legs. I brought the brush forward and smeared the concoction onto her bare skin. The girl's eyes shot open. Her slender hand clutched mine, gripping with surprising strength.

From the corner of my vision, I saw the horde converge. Already the illusion had taken hold of the boy. Instead of a slumbering body, he now appeared as a pile of cast offs from a butcher.

The girl fixed me with her gaze. The pupils expanded, obliterating the iris. It felt like staring into a black pond where the cold water ran deep. The more I looked, the more I was lost in the intensity of her eyes.

"I shall devour you," she said and grinned her needle smile.

The scrabble of motion. Bodies closing in around me.

I snatched the brush with my other hand and slapped the wet bristles against the girl's skin.

84

She laughed, a maniacal light glinting from her eyes. "Nothing can hurt me."

I kept plastering the concoction on and the illusion transformed where it struck. Gone was the girl's lithe form, replaced with dripping offal and entrails.

"I shall burn this world!" She wailed.

The villagers pressed inward. I abandoned the brush and crawled back. All around, the sounds of smacking lips, the clacking of teeth. Distended bellies brushed against my shoulders.

I scrambled away and could no longer see the children. Only the clump of the villagers, pressing inward.

The boy had awoken, grunting and squealing, perhaps mimicking the sounds of the slaughtered stag. But the girl went on laughing. I caught snippets of words, the clearest being "Forever."

The wreckage of my house was now cleared. All the villagers massed together over the hearth, forming a hillock of writhing, biting, chewing bodies. I located my spade and began to toss fresh earth over the horde. For every shovelful of dirt I scooped up, their flailing arms knocked most of it away. Yet I did not worry that they should break free from their feast. I had arranged an inexhaustible food source, a perfect match to their hunger. The children would repair every injury, only to have another chunk of flesh bitten off.

It took all day, scooping dirt from the perimeter of the clearing. Now a barrow mound greeted me where once my cottage stood. I patted the sides with the shovel, smoothing and compressing the earth. The sun hung low and thin tree-shadows cut across the hill of earth like black stripes.

I pressed one ear to the side of the mound and at first heard nothing. But then, distant, packed under the weight of dirt, came the gnashing of teeth and the grunting from the boy. And still, the girl's laughter. All of these muffled by the heady loam of earth. The sound would keep on and on. Because, as the girl said, nothing could truly harm her. Her kind of evil can never truly be defeated.

Only buried for a time.

But never forgotten.

SNAP

BRENNAN LAFARO

"Ah, Mr. Perkins, how are you this fine morning?"
"Quite good. Quite good, my dear Mr. Jeffries. A
fine Monday, this." The rotund man plopped into a chair at
the conference table. Mr. Jeffries was already seated and
waiting.

"Indeed, but aren't they all?"

Mr. Perkins tented his fingers and leaned onto the table.
"Did you have a good weekend?"

"Dreadful. And yourself?"

"Positively the same. Say, did you hear about Leonard?
Manager from the shipping floor?"

"No, I'm afraid not. He's a good worker as I recall." Mr.
Jeffries frowned.

"Excellent worker, very productive. Heart attack. In the
cardiac I.C.U. the better part of the weekend."

"Back today?"

"No, his wife called in for him. Says if he pulls through he
won't be in for at least a week. Likely longer."

"A week? No, no, no. That's no good."

"The order for Abraxas Industries is due to ship out

tomorrow afternoon. Like you say, simply unacceptable. We'll have to get a new man in here right away."

Mr. Jeffries shook his head. "We're at full capacity, can't go on a hiring spree. Union will pitch an absolute fit."

"Hm, hold on." Mr. Perkins closed his eyes and gave a quick snap of the fingers.

"Okay, that's settled." A sly grin slid across Mr. Jeffries' face. "Have your laptop?"

"Of course." Mr. Perkins put his device on the table, opened it, and logged in.

"Get a listing up for a new shipping floor manager. 40 hours a week, no overtime. Salary to be conditional to experience. Emphasize that they must start immediately."

Mr. Perkins tapped furiously at the keyboard while Mr. Jeffries slurped his coffee.

"Done." Mr. Perkins wrung his hands off, warding away potential onset carpal tunnel.

The phone rang.

"Ah," said Mr. Jeffries. Both men lunged for the phone, but Mr. Jeffries was faster. "Perhaps our first applicant. Hello?"

Mr. Perkins strained to listen as an unintelligible drone sounded on the other end of the line.

"I'm sorry, I can't quite understand you. I see. Yes, of course. Thank you. And you, my dear."

Mr. Jeffries hung up. "That was Mrs. Leonard. Her husband passed away a few minutes ago, complications from heart disease. Curious that she should dial us up so quickly, don't you think?"

"Well," said Mr. Perkins, "when I spoke with her on Saturday, I was *quite* insistent about keeping us updated. It's a good thing we've been proactive about finding his replacement."

The two men stared at each other then burst into laughter, Mr. Perkins nearly fell out of his seat.

The phone rang, and this time Mr. Perkins reached it first.

"Yes? Perfect. No, I trust your judgment, Ms. Elliot. Oh no, immediately. Within the hour I should say. Perfect."

He hung up.

"We have our replacement. A man named Walsh is on his way as we speak to take over the shipping floor."

"Everything is moving like clockwork then. All orders set to go out in a timely fashion?"

"Every last one."

A gleam flickered in Mr. Jeffries' eye. "Shall we discuss our wager?"

"Yes, let's."

Mr. Jeffries took a ledger from his coat pocket. "At last count, I am ahead 531 to 517."

"Ah, you may have the upper hand, but Mr. Leonard brings me to 518."

"Correct you are, sir." Mr. Jeffries added a mark in the ledger.

"Today is what? 23rd of the month?"

"It is indeed. Thirty-eight days left in the year. Can you make up the deficit?"

Mr. Perkins snapped his fingers, a muffled scream sounded through the open door of the conference room. "Oh yes, I think I'll be quite alright."

Mr. Jeffries clucked his tongue and his eyes clouded over. "Don't be hasty, friend. Two positions to fill in just one day?"

"Do you really think we'll have trouble getting someone new in? In this economy?"

Mr. Jeffries leaned in and lowered his voice. "Do you even know who that was?"

"Davis in accounting."

"A fine worker. Why him?"

"A fine worker, yes, but a bit of a prick. He tends to flip us the bird, as they say, when he thinks we are unaware."

"The bird, eh? He was always nice to me," mused Mr. Jeffries. "Well good riddance, I suppose."

The door burst open.

"Mr. Jeffries! Mr. Perkins!" A short, thin, blonde woman stood in the doorway, out of breath. Her face was flushed, whether from shock or exertion, neither man could guess. "There's been an accident. Davis... in accounting. It's... there's so much blood." She sucked in deep breaths between words.

Mr. Jeffries stood up. "Ms. Elliot, whatever are you doing here? Call an ambulance at once!"

Ms. Elliot stood framed in the doorway a moment longer, looking as though she wanted to argue, then thought better of it, and disappeared.

Already on his feet, Mr. Jeffries walked over to shut the door. "A little too flashy, I think. What did you do to the man, anyway?"

Mr. Perkins grinned in response, the corners of his mouth edging close to his ears. His exposed teeth appeared pointed.

Mr. Jeffries shook his head. "No matter."

The two men worked at their laptops in silence until interrupted by the wailing of sirens. The ambulance painted the walls of the conference room in shades of blue and red. They exchanged the occasional look, but didn't resume their discussions until after Davis had been taken away. The lights still flashed as the ambulance departed, but the sirens didn't make a sound.

"519," said Mr. Perkins. "Mark it down."

Mr. Jeffries sighed, removing the ledger from his coat pocket again, he struck another tally. "519," he repeated.

"Is that ad for accounting posted?"

"Yes, with 'Start immediately' printed in the byline."

"Very good. Would you prefer to wait for the call or perform the ten o'clock staff inspection?"

"I think it would be wise for me to run inspections today. I love a good culling as much as the next demon, but think of how we got to these numbers, Mr. Perkins."

Mr. Perkins' eyes flashed a glowing red, then settled. He flicked his tongue to the side of his mouth before speaking. "You are right, my friend. Patience."

"Patience and care, Mr. Perkins." Mr. Jeffries stood up and straightened his tie. "Two is a lot for one day, but rest assured. I'll be keeping track." He patted his coat pocket where he had returned the ledger. "The shirkers, the ones who abuse their sick days, the liars, and the cheaters. Their tickets are punched. They just don't know it yet." Mr. Jeffries exited the room, leaving Mr. Perkins to wait by a phone which refused to ring.

Mr. Perkins stared at his right thumb, resting against his middle finger. Surely, one more snap couldn't hurt anything. Right?

EATING INTO YOUR FREE TIME

DEREK DES ANGES

Amber Houghton had never contemplated spitting in someone else's drink before. It was one of those really gross, unhygienic, litigation-worthy things people sometimes reported on the news which made her keep an eagle-eyed watch on people when she could afford to order a coffee somewhere else. Almost, but not quite, as diligently as she watched people around her drinks at bars—where the stakes were higher, and a lot worse.

But she'd never had to work at GalaxyQuids Coffee chain before now, either.

"I have never wanted to poison anyone in my life before," said Binni, cutting through her thoughts as he came out of the bathroom with a paper towel roll in his hands, "but if one more customer yells at me about the Cinnamon Buckup Star I will put bleach in their drink."

Amber passed him her till card. "I was going to go with spitting," she confessed, "but I've only been yelled at three times today. How many does it take for bleach?"

Binni spread the fingers of his free hand into a broad,

light-brown starfish of exasperation. "One more and I qualify for a talking-to."

"I'm not sure how you're supposed to solve their *emotional problems* by getting given some of your own," Amber sighed, sliding into the bathroom in a gap only just large enough for her body.

As she went, the familiar sound of a customer "demanding their rights" rose up above the hubbub of conversation at the tables. "WELL I ALWAYS HAVE THAT ONE, AND I DON'T SEE WHY—"

———

ANY SMUGNESS AMBER might have felt at being behind on the Being Yelled At By Customers ranking—roughly none— evaporated over the course of the next shift.

It started normally enough: she hid her long black hair under the hairnet and "Happy To Serve You" hat that came with the uniform, spent 25 minutes *before* clock-in time cleaning the bathroom because if they did it on-shift it counted as "slacking," and told the new hire that her make-up looked nice.

And then they opened, two minutes past 7:00 A.M., and everything *immediately* went to shit.

First, while she was mixing a previous order, a woman in a Chanel suit barked at her like a dog for not answering a question that sounded like it was being addressed into the very obvious and somewhat outdated bluetooth earpiece sticking out of her ear; then the customer she'd been mixing the order for shouted at her for not getting it fast enough; and *then*, bringing her ahead of Binni's ranking, a *third* customer called her an uppity bitch for telling her which non-dairy milks the branch did and didn't carry.

"Please tell me I win some kind of prize for this," Amber

said, when the morning rush was over, and the shift manager, Phillipe, had finished tallying up everyone's Getting Yelled At By Customers totals on their very-much-out-of-sight-of-the-customers whiteboard.

"You win... a visit by Kevin Bridgens," said Phillipe, putting the whiteboard away.

Amber knew exactly who this was, because his portrait was in the office-*cum*-supply-cupboard, next to the bathroom. He had a face like the offspring of a boiled ham and a thirty-years-buried cadaver, the only man she'd ever seen who managed to look both gaunt and porky at the same time. A rictus grin of self-satisfaction, a pink shirt, a blue jacket, and dead eyes, all at a "flattering" three-quarter angle against the mandatory beige corporate background.

He owned every single GalaxyQuids in the region, a super franchisee who, she was reliably informed, had once bought a pink yacht by accident and instead of repainting it, bought a second one and gave the first to his mistress.

As Amber had sold her graduation necklace to pay her rent the week that she found that out, she hadn't found it particularly funny.

"Because of me?" she asked, too tired to think straight as she closed the office door behind them.

Phillipe gave her a pitying look. "No, Amber. He's coming anyway. Annual inspection. He's a"—here he rolled his big green eyes and gesticulated incoherently—"*hands-on* kinda guy."

Hands-on was, in Amber's eyes, a red flag. *Hands-on* men were the kind who couldn't be trusted with your drink in a bar.

"Great," she said, forcing a smile onto her face as another customer wandered in with a tiny dog under her arm, despite the *no dogs* sign. "Superb."

BECAUSE MR. BRIDGENS-CALL-ME-KEV was coming the next day, everyone had to work after clock-out to make sure the branch was *spotless*, that everything was in its franchise-mandated place, regardless of how stupid or inconvenient or unsafe that was, and that the syrups were properly on display—even though that meant they immediately dripped on the floor, where they had to be constantly mopped up.

While they were doing this, another four people came and banged on the door, screaming some version of *I know you're open* despite the very large sign reading: *Sorry! We're Closed! Call Back Again Soon!*

When the alarm went off the next morning, and Amber rolled over on the sofa-bed and thought very passionately about taking a sick day despite the loss of cash, the sun was just rising.

It spilled an unearthly, slightly menacing red across the bins as she closed the garden gate behind her. As far as she could remember, that meant it was going to rain later, which meant damp, miserable customers, and a lot more yelling.

Great.

First, her job made her too tired to have hobbies. Then it ate up her time and made her too tired to look for any *other* jobs. And *then* the customers ate into her will to live by being universally horrible.

She arrived under the same baleful light, and hastily shut the door behind her in case any of them tried to break in.

Binni greeted her with a mop in his hands and uttered the immortal words, "Guess how hard it is to get congealed syrup off the floor when it's been there for hours?"

"Have you tried bleach?" Amber asked, putting on her hair net as someone peered in through the window.

"Amber my love, I've tried everything short of black magic."

"Was that next on the list?" Amber asked, putting on her hat. The red dawn light had alleviated to an ugly orange and came in through the window at exactly the right angle to get in her eyes.

"Nah," Binni said, shading his eyes with his arm. "Mr. Bridgens is already descending on us. I don't want to summon the devil as well."

———

BEFORE THE ARRIVAL of the man Bini referred to as their "end of level" boss, "because he's the one you have to beat to escape", they still had customers to deal with.

Within almost seconds of opening the door, all the work they'd done the night before was undone in a hurricane of dirty shoes; violent toddlers with a proprietary attitude towards snacks that weren't, strictly speaking, theirs; and a vomiting jogger who at least had the decency to be mortified by his attack of stomach failure, although not enough to stick around and help them wipe the floor.

"If these are omens," Bini said darkly, toeing blue paper towels across a sea of disinfectant soap and trying to fend off incomers with the *wet floor* sign, "I don't like the look of them."

"Don't let it get to you," Philippe said, not very convincingly.

"What about the fact that people usually leave after an *interview* with Mr Bridgens? Can I let that get to me instead?" Binni muttered, plastering on a fake smile as two middle-aged women in athleisure gear strolled in with reusable cups at the ready.

"What?" Amber whispered, throwing the milk foaming

nozzle in the sink haphazardly and replacing it with a ready-steamed one. It was still a little too hot to touch, but she'd just about got the calluses on her hand from last time, so it didn't hurt as much.

"I just assumed it's because he's such a *dick*," Binni hissed, scuttling past with the wet paper towels, "that no one can withstand being in private with him."

———

Mr. Bridgens-Call-Me-Kev and his ingratiating smirk arrived during the lunch rush, because, really, when else would he have turned up?

Amber clocked him coming in through the door behind two over-groomed women in designer coats; he was very clearly checking them out. He made eye-contact with her just as the customer at the counter—a tall, thin, white man in a grey suit with his hair fleeing from his temples like it was embarrassed to be seen with him—told her she was incompetent, which was exactly what Amber felt the day had really been lacking so far.

She forced a smile onto her face and apologised to the customer, trying very hard to keep an eye on the spreading puddle of syrup under nozzles, and to make sure that Binni didn't collide with Phillippe as one took the next order and the other tried to make three of the last ones at once.

As the line moved forward Amber's chest squeezed around her heart like a nervous fist choking the life out of some unlucky cockroach. Somewhere in the back of her heard a nature documentary narration started up, something about the Big Predator on the plains stalking a herd of gazelle.

Of course, she didn't really have the time to watch docu-

mentaries any more, so for all she knew the guy who
narrated them normally had died.

Amber winced. The line moved down.

Mr Bridgens-Call-Me-Kev broke out of the line and
wandered around the shop, looking at the framed pictures
on the walls which Amber had spent far too long the night
before dusting; at the unoccupied tables which she hadn't
had a chance to sponge down since the last customers threw
hot chocolate over them; at the open door to the bathroom
which plainly displayed they hadn't had a chance to fill in the
hygiene inspection box for ten that morning.

Every so often he shot glances over at the tills, still smiling,
with his hands in the pockets of his expensive jeans. He was
wearing them with a blazer which, in Amber's estimation,
would probably cost about six to eight months of her full-time
wages—not, of course, that she ever got scheduled for the full
number of hours per week that would let her get sick pay.
Full-time was poison in Mr. Bridgens-Call-Me-Kev's mouth.

The second time he caught her eye he raised his
eyebrows. His blandly normal, came-with-the-frame face
was the absolute portrait of an area manager, but unfortunately the portrait was one that was probably on a watchlist
somewhere.

Amber tried very, very hard to stop her smile from
calcifying.

She wasn't really sure it had worked.

"Amber," he said, from beside one of the customers, his
hands still in his pockets and making a distressing denim
tent out of the front of his jeans, "time for a chat in the office,
when you have a minute."

His smile seemed perfectly genuine, and genuinely
unpleasant.

Amber suppressed a shudder, and nodded.

The moment stretched on forever in front of her.

Amber's neck grew hot with the gazes of the customers staring at her. She didn't bother to take off her apron, just took a deep and steadying breath before she stepped around the counter and crossed the floor to the office door ahead of Mr. Bridgens.

He extended a polite arm in front to indicate she should go in front.

It wasn't even a *big* branch of GalaxyQuids, and somehow it felt like it was the size of a stadium by the time her fingers closed on the office door.

She wasn't really sure if getting out of the sight of the customers was a relief: the part of her that was thinking of saving up for a taser for late night commutes whispered something about him not being able to "try anything" if she was in public, but she hushed it.

It wasn't like Amber wanted to get a dressing-down in front of people she'd have to smile at later.

The door made a protesting noise that wrenched an answering leap out of her pulse, and finally she was inside.

The office felt bigger than it usually did, because they'd taken out all the inventory and crammed it into the cupboard behind the bathroom—and god help them if Mr. Bridgens looked in there—but it still was not much bigger than the bathroom itself.

So it wasn't really a surprise, Amber thought as she inched surreptitiously away from Mr. Bridgens, that she felt the same way as when she got into a lift and the only other person in there was a man who smelled really strongly of aftershave and had loafers on with no socks; groomed for arrogance and aggressive heterosexuality. A bit like the way she imagined a fish felt, when it realised that the shimmering thing around it wasn't one it could escape through: cornered.

Her pulse was probably in the triple figures now. She

tried to strike a balance between a polite smile and not
looking like she was in any way encouraging the inevitable,
but Amber had the feeling it came out looking like she was
holding back sick.

She hoped like hell he was only planning on yelling at her.

Mr. Bridgens shook his head, gave her a small smile, and
leaned over to close the door. It was probably only because
the office was so small that he leaned near enough she could
almost feel him on her arm hairs, which were all standing
on end.

He seemed unusually cold for someone that nearby, but
she didn't get so much as a second to think about it.

She watched him lock the door with mounting pressure
squeezing at her chest. The distance between him and a
reasonable distance to stand away from people you weren't
dating was already into negative inches.

"Amber," said Mr. Bridgens, somehow contriving to fill
up the space between the door, the hastily-cleaned desk, and
herself almost totally, despite the physical impossibility of
that. He didn't seem like the kind of man who did things like
that by accident. They wrote whole books about how to have
Alpha Posture, after all. "Amber, Amber, Amber."

Amber tried to give him her best Customer Service Smile
and to not think about how the office didn't have a window.

"Mr. Bridgens," she said, in case that was the answer he
was looking for.

It wasn't.

He was standing obnoxiously close. The blazer smelled of
aftershave, except towards the collar, where it smelled of hair
spray. It was far from the worst thing she'd smelled at work
that week, but it gave her more creeping dread than even the
overflowing toilet had. His hands rested, briefly, on his belt.
Amber began to feel sick.

Mr. Bridgens shook his head again with a rueful little

smile, and the spiel began. "Amber, you know, I started this business with nothing—"

Nothing was a funny way to describe a £100,000 loan from his parents, in Amber's opinion, but maybe it looked like nothing to him now.

"—and I got where I am now through *hard work*. Hard work, Amber. Hard work and ensuring that the customer is *always* satisfied. Never cutting corners. Never wasting time, or money. And I expect this same level of dedication from my staff, Amber."

Mr. Bridgens undid his blazer button as he went on; Amber found she'd backed up so far that the wall display was digging into the back strap of her bra.

"Uh-huh," she said. She didn't really want to think about her bra, in case it somehow made *him* think about her bra, although she was pretty sure, given how close he was to her, he was probably already thinking about it.

He undid the top button of his shirt collar. "And I can't help but notice, Amber, that you're not giving one hundred percent out there. You're letting standards slip. My customers expect better than this, Amber."

"Sorry, Mr Bridgens," Amber said, struggling valiantly to avoid both his eyes and the fact that he had just undone another two of his buttons.

"You're going to have to do better, Amber," Mr. Bridgens said, as Amber slowly unfocused her eyes so she wouldn't have to look right at him. "I don't pay you to give me second-best performance. I pay you people enough as it is, you know that? The cost of staffing these franchises is *ludicrous*."

Even under the increasing tide of discomfort over how many of the Regional Owner's shirt buttons were currently undone, Amber couldn't help thinking that the *ludicrous cost* to Mr. Bridgens wasn't exactly keeping her in diamond rings. She couldn't even afford her own room.

She tried to back further away, but the wall was in the way.

"The question is," Mr. Bridgens asked, his shirt now hanging entirely open, "what are we going to do with you?"

Amber was mustering up the courage to whisper the words *nothing unless you want a sexual harassment lawsuit,* knowing full well she couldn't afford a lawyer, when she actually *looked* between the dangling flaps of expensive pink cotton and their pearlescent buttons.

What she saw knocked the words—all words—clean out of her head.

A hubcap-sized tunnel lay in the middle of Mr. Bridgens' torso, fringed with rows and rows and rows of tiny, needle-point teeth, all pointing inward down the impossibly long hole. It seemed to go on far deeper than his body did. Above it blinked a row of around eight eyes—she wasn't really in the mood for counting—like glittering black jewels sunk into the skin, which seemed to be sliding off like an ill-fitting rubber glove.

"Fuck," Amber whispered. All the blood drained from her face; her lips went numb.

"See," said Mr. Bridgens, out of the physics-bending carnivorous void in his middle, "this is why I can't have you talking to customers. You've got a foul mouth."

He stepped closer again.

SUFFER THE CHILDREN
LAUREL HIGHTOWER

"Now I recognize, employees have lives beyond this company. You all have families that place needs on you, and I'm here to tell you I'm no different. My wife and I raised two brilliant daughters to adulthood together, so I understand the strains and demands of parenting. But I'm proud to say, in my 27 years as C.E.O. of this firm, I've never once brought my children to work, or missed because they were ill. I expect the same kind of commitment out of you."

Tony Westruther stared out into a sea of strangers, relishing the silence that greeted his words. These were the new recruits, and he always made it his business to address them on their first day. It helped set expectations early, and if any of them complained later, he could say with perfect truth that they'd known from day one what their priorities were. He knew people didn't like it, thought his company should be one of those namby pamby places like Google where the staff rode slides into meetings and families participated. Fuck that. If you gave people an inch, they'd steal a mile, so Tony operated under the adage that no inches were given.

He straightened his tie, shot the cuffs of the shirt his wife had pressed for him that morning. She was using too much starch again, and he made a mental note to tell her.

"My hope is, we can start with open and honest communication, and continue that way. We all know what to expect from one another, and I look forward to a long, fulfilling relationship with each of you."

The lights came on in the conference room and people began to shuffle to their feet. This group was quieter than most— he was used to whispering, a bit of outrage in response to his remarks, but not one of the new hires said a word. He surveyed them with approval. Men, almost every one of them, which explained it. He smiled. This was going to work out fine.

As he gathered his jacket and phone, his gaze fell on the sole female occupant of the room. She stood by the door, as though she were ushering the others out, and her eyes were on him. Her expression was calm and easy, her demeanor professional. He noted with satisfaction that she was older, which meant menopause and grown kids, if any. Perfect. Maternity leave was the bane of his existence, not to mention the price hike breeding-age women caused to health insurance premiums.

Tony strode down the halls of the third floor, passing through the cubicle farm, fixing a smile of vague friendliness on his face while making certain to avoid eye contact with anyone. Things were quiet out here in the call center today, too, which was odd. He cast a glance over his shoulder as he reached the executive elevator, and stopped. The cubes were empty. Not a soul answering phones. The center was staffed twenty-four hours a day, seven days a week, with minimum wage workers that came and went on an endless conveyor belt. It was always noisy down here, but today there was only silence.

He frowned. Was there a training he hadn't known about?
A fire drill? Or heaven forbid, some kind of employee appre-
ciation event? But even then, the call center staff was
required to go in shifts, so it didn't make sense. He'd have to
have a talk with the staffing manager. Things were getting
too lax for his liking, especially on a day with so many new
recruits starting. He didn't want them getting the impression
they could laze about.

The elevator dinged and he stepped inside, relaxing as
the gold plated walls swished shut before him. It was a
burden to have to be "on" all the time, but that was part of
the job. Tony Westruther was an image as much as he was an
institution.

The bell chimed and the doors slid open on the second
floor. He frowned at the woman who stepped inside. It was
the one from the meeting, the old lady. What the hell was she
doing here? This was the executive elevator. He wondered if
he could have made a mistake, failed to recognize one of his
senior staffers. He didn't think so, but there was always a
possibility she could be visiting from another franchise
office. He didn't want to make an ass of himself by questioning her, so he returned her generic smile and pulled out
his phone, stepping back to let her go first when the door
opened.

He was halfway down the plush hallway that led to his
office suite before he realized the woman was keeping pace
with him. He cast another glance her way, but she didn't
seem to be paying attention to him, so maybe she knew
where she was going.

The third floor was quiet as well, he thought as he passed
a stretch of offices that should have been full of chattering
sales people. The thick carpets along the hallways muffled
the noise somewhat, but the silence was eerie. Tony peered
in each office as he passed, and saw that none were occupied.

He stopped, and the woman kept going, which was at least one annoyance off his back.

He poked his head into the office of one of his V.P.'s, Jeff Magnum. The guy lived for his job, was a hell of a sales rep, and never missed a day of work that wasn't planned at least six months in advance. But his chair was empty, his computer monitor dark, and his coffee pot cold.

Tony stepped back out into the empty hallway and listened. Nothing. Not a single phone, voice, or footstep. Where the hell was everyone?

"Jeff? Barry? Glenda? Anybody up here?"

More silence answered him, and he thinned his lips. If this turned out to be some kind of prank, heads would roll. Tony was good for a laugh or two, but not on company time, and sure as shit not with this kind of lapse in productivity. He started down toward his office again.

"Glenda?" If anyone was here, it would be his personal secretary. Even if the rest of them were in on some elaborate prank, she'd never join in. In fact, he was ninety percent certain she'd rat the rest of them out.

He straightened his tie and lifted his chin. Glenda was the answer to this, and once he'd dealt with whatever it was, he could get back to work.

But Glenda's desk was empty, her desk light switched off. Tony turned, looking everywhere. He was alone.

No, not entirely alone. The door to his own office was open, and he could see a shadow within. He hesitated outside the door, his heart beat uncomfortably loud in his ears. An intruder? Or was it something less sinister—a surprise party, maybe? His birthday wasn't for months, but his hiring anniversary had just passed, maybe that's what this was about.

He smiled, his confidence restored. Of course, a surprise.

Tony was a good boss, the kind of man of the people that won him admirers throughout the staff. It made sense they'd want to do something special for him. "You guys," he said as he pushed the door open, but the words died on his lips.

The only person in his office was the old woman, the one who'd been in the elevator. She was sitting in his chair, and she smiled again when he walked in. He realized uneasily that it wasn't a very nice smile. It was rather cold, and there was something behind it he didn't like.

"You want to tell me who you are, and what you're doing in my office?" He tried to keep his tone easy and light—there was still the possibility she'd been sent by corporate.

She inclined her head. "I'm Mother. And I'm waiting."

Her voice made him feel strange. Small, and ashamed, though there was nothing in her tone but gentility. Maybe she reminded him of someone.

He shook it off. "Waiting for what?"

Her smile widened until it stretched to obscene size, consuming her face beneath it.

"For that," she said at the same time a piercing, head split-ting shriek made Tony clap his hands over his ears.

He felt like someone had shoved an ice pick in both ears. "What the fuck *is* that?" he shouted.

The woman stood and stepped out from behind his desk, her smile back to normal, and much warmer. She chuckled as she passed him. "We forget so quickly, don't we? How those newborn cries can sound?"

She brushed him on her way out the door and he recoiled from her touch. Fury bubbling up in his chest, he strode out into the hall, determined to have it out with whoever had brought a baby to work, on the executive floor no less.

He stopped before he reached Glenda's empty desk, pulled up short by the sight that greeted him. The third floor, which moments before had been empty, was filled with wall to wall people. None of them were ones he recognized, and they were all staring at him, completely silent.

Except that was wrong on both counts. He realized he knew some of these faces, even if only vaguely. They were the newbies, the kids downstairs he'd just been addressing. And one of them was the source of that godawful racket.

Tony drew himself up to full height, about to let loose on these assholes. Fired, every last one of them, for this bullshit prank. But there was something about the sight of a fully grown man in a suit crying like a hysterical newborn – he just couldn't make himself speak. As he watched, more mouths opened, more cries began. Soon the entire group had their heads thrown back, caterwauling, while that crazy old lady stood by looking, what, wistful?

"What the hell is this?" he shouted, but his words were swallowed. His hands remained clamped over his ears, but there was that strange disturbance of air that happens with human voices over a certain decibel, the effect that sounds almost like a zipper. His headache intensified, and his vision wavered.

Which accounted for how long it took him to notice when the men – boys – began changing. It happened in a sort of domino effect throughout the group. One threw his head back, his throat working in agonized ripples, until the flesh around it began to bubble. Smoke rose from the collars and sleeves of jackets, the cuffs of pants, and Tony watched, jaw dropped and nausea churning his stomach, as the boys appeared to melt. Their clothes puddled around them as their bodies reduced, a choking gurgling replacing the cries. And still, the woman stood over them, smiling down, as though she wasn't witnessing a mass casualty.

When it was over, the wet choking sounds quieted, smoke

rising around fleshy lumps under piles of empty clothes, the stench that rose made Tony move his hands from his ears to his nose and mouth, but still it coated his tongue, pushed its way back down his throat. He gagged, dropping to his knees.

"What is all of this?" he asked the woman, who seemed unaffected, looking fondly down at the gobs of melted flesh. "What did you do to them?"

She lifted her gaze to meet his. "I gave them life. I brought them this far, now it's your turn."

"*What?* Who are you?"

"I'm Mother," she said, with another flash of that smile that was so very wrong. She bent to give the closest smoking pile a loving pat, then reached behind her for a purse, settled it onto her shoulder and began to walk away.

Tony stared at what remained of his newest class of recruits, wondering how the hell to explain this. Under his gaze, the piles of flesh began to move. He moaned and scrambled away until his back hit the wall behind Glenda's desk. There was a sickly squelching that accompanied the writhing, then a wet *pop* as one fell apart.

Within, blinking at Tony with round, black eyes, was a newborn baby. Wrinkled and covered in unspeakable fluids, it kicked its legs, and then it began to scream.

More wet pops sounded from the other mounds, and more screaming began.

Tony got to his feet, hands at his sides, his tie and hair askew. There was no one here but him. He looked up and saw the woman's shadow disappearing toward the elevator bank, and began to run after her.

"Wait—where are you going? What am I supposed to do with all these things?"

She didn't turn back, but he heard her voice lilting down the elevator shaft. "I have to work, Mr. Westruther. But you've raised two daughters to adulthood, and with never a day off. I'm sure you're up to the challenge."

As the echo of her words died away, the screaming of the babies filled his ears. The lights that lined the hallway blinked off one by one, and he was alone, in the dark, with the children.

ON PROBATION
DONALD MCCARTHY

"That's not what happened," Rosa protests, knowing it's pointless, knowing she'll hate herself if she says nothing.

Jonathan Grammell offers a sigh in response. His face is shadowed since the office's light is dim and outside are only clouds. "It doesn't matter," he says. There might be consolation in his voice; it might also be condescension. "If the client says it happened one way, then, for all intents and purposes, that's the way it happened." His hands are folded on his desk as he speaks, which reminds Rosa of a teacher she had in the second grade who would never raise her voice when scolding students.

"I am very sorry," Rosa says, not for the first time nor even the fifth. All of this over the fact that yesterday a man in a three-piece suit collided with her while she cleaned the hallway. The man in the three-piece suit did not see the incident so innocently, claiming Rosa ignored his polite requests to move. Rosa cannot say the man lied, of course, so she struggles for kinder wording. "Maybe the client misunderstood what happened."

Grammell puts his hand up to stop her. He's young, not yet forty, which makes it worse: he'll be with the company as long as Rosa, and this will hang over every interaction they have, provided she keeps her job. This would not be the first time she's lost a position thanks to forces outside of her control. "You need to understand that the defense industry is a tricky business," says Grammell. "Clients can be, oh, let's go with mercurial." He pauses for a moment, and Rosa half expects he's waiting for her to ask what that word means. He continues, "So, it just won't do to have you on this floor when he comes back, and, since he'll be coming back a bit for the next couple of weeks, I think it'd be best if you were stationed elsewhere." He leans back in his chair and crosses his arms against his broad chest. "I'm thinking floor fifteen, HR. George resigned a week ago, so Marcia can use a second hand down there during the day."

She feels tiny in her chair, even tinier than usual, and her voice has so little strength today. "I can do that. I'd be happy to." It's a busier floor, more work without a doubt, but she'll still be getting her paycheck. Two minutes ago she felt uncertain if she'd ever see a check from Tyrius Incorporated again. She cannot go looking for another job once more. She'd crack.

"Very good," Grammell says. He holds up an index finger. "There is one other thing. You will be put on probation. Not for long, just a bureaucratic thing, the client made some noise is all, so we want to be able to tell him action was taken. You can just check the company app on your phone, and it will let you know when you're no longer on probation. You do fine down in HR, and it'll be removed in no time. Then you can come back up here and all will be right."

———

THE PROTESTORS SCREAM OUTSIDE Tyrius Incorporated again. Earlier, one of them threw a balloon filled with animal blood against the front doors and was hauled away by the police. The blood still leaks down the door when Rosa leaves work. She wraps her coat around herself, looks down at the ground, and hurries past the commotion, hoping she won't be noticed. She's short, so she can usually avoid attention. "You're neither desirable nor objectionable," her sister, now dead of pancreatic cancer, once told her.

Tyrius' skyscraper, the tallest in the City, looms over her as she leaves. A shiny black slab planted in the middle of the City, as if the architect was less interested in aesthetic pleasure than in a symbol of power, the Tyrius skyscraper is unmistakable. On her first day of work, Rosa found the sight overwhelming but inspiring. Now, she finds it bleak, resembling an elaborate grave marker.

A moment before Rosa turns the block to go to the subway, an older woman grabs her and says, "How does it feel working for Murder Incorporated?"

"I'm just part of the cleaning crew," Rosa tells her. The old woman is sickly pale, but her eyes are bright blue and angry, their judgment fierce. "Please let me go."

The old woman does, but snaps, "You must know what goes on in there. I used to work for Tyrius. Seventeen years. One day I heard their victims' voices; one day, I heard their screams. I bet you've heard them, too. Have some self-respect for yourself and quit."

"I'd go broke if I quit," Rosa replies. "I'm trapped." This isn't the first time she's faced jeers while leaving work. She's not sure there's a point in trying to convince the woman, but, like earlier with Grammell, she cannot stay silent.

"You're disgusting," the old woman says. "You're Hispanic, right? When the US sends death squads down to Latin America, what company gives them the guns? Yours!"

Rosa hurries to the subway, half-wishing she was fired today, half-wishing she had the backbone to quit. If only she had money. Similar thoughts bothered her when she worked for a coat manufacturing company that used child labor overseas. That job spit her out when costs needed to be cut.

———

ROSA PUSHES the cordless power mop across the men's room floor. She's forced to go over the restroom three times before she's satisfied, although that sense of satisfaction will be brief. The floor will soon be marred once more, since lunch break begins in an hour.

She retreats to the breakroom for her ten-minute respite. The room is cramped, with one table, two rickety chairs, and a microwave that is only capable of turning food lukewarm. She takes out her phone and opens the Tyrius app. It greets her with the word WELCOME in elaborate font. The screen goes black for a moment and then a picture of Rosa appears in the right corner. She looks younger in it even though it was taken only a few months ago. She's smiling in the picture, and her face is full. She's lost some weight recently, and she's not sure why. The bones in her face are more prominent now. In the picture, her black hair is down; now, she keeps it pulled tightly back, so tight someone once asked if it hurt.

Below her image is her ID number. Below that is her status, which currently says ON PROBATION.

It is not a surprise to see it there, but anxiety still crawls over her. Despite Grammell's assurances that it meant nothing, probation meant the slightest mistake would result in termination. She tries to justify it in her head, remembering Grammell saying he had to do something to placate the client. The probation has nothing to do with her, not really, and it seemed like Grammell liked her judging by their conversation. In that case, what is there to worry about?

Well, maybe a lot considering the morality of the people she's working for, considering what they create, considering how disposable she must look to them. These poisonous thoughts come on quick, and she does her best to shove them away.

The door to the breakroom opens, forcing Rosa to stay in the present, to think rationally. Her new coworker, Marcia, steps in. Marcia is long past retirement age and always seems to be sighing. Rosa is sure there's a story behind why Marcia still has to work, but she can only hear so many of those stories before she breaks.

"Glad to have an extra pair of hands around here," Marcia says, sitting. She's a large woman, but strong. Her hair is gray and full.

"I'm just down here for a bit," Rosa murmurs.

"That's what George said a year ago," Marcia replies. "He was still here a week back when he got a new job. I think it paid less, but he said he was tired of toilets. I say, whether it's a toilet, a chair, or a floor, cleaning something is cleaning something. Hey, you speak English fine, right? I don't need to slow down when I talk to you?"

Rosa balks at the question. "I don't speak anything other than English."

"No Spanish at all? Where were you born then?"

"Here."

"In the City?" Marcia shrugs. "That's too bad. Probably be nice to have a memory of somewhere else." She takes a salad out of her bag and begins to shovel in forkfuls of lettuce, apparently done with conversation.

Rosa checks her status again. ON PROBATION. She's not sure why she expected it would have changed. She tells herself this is different from her last layoff. In fact, this is not a layoff at all, so that word should not be in her mind. She tries to banish it, but it sneaks back in soon enough.

———

ON PROBATION. ON PROBATION. ON PROBATION. ON PROBATION. ON PROBATION.

———

"Mr. Grammell is not in," says the secretary. He does not look at Rosa. Instead, he stares at his computer, which currently displays a social media website, and breathes just sharply enough to let Rosa know he's annoyed. It's not necessary. His horn-rimmed glasses already do the job of projecting that he is perpetually aggravated, but it's clear to Rosa that his level of contempt for her is deep.

"I want to speak with him for only a minute," she says. She leans down, placing her hands on the secretary's desk.

"Hands off," he snaps. "Mr. Grammell is not in. He won't be in all day. I'll let him know you stopped by. If he has the time, he will come and find you."

"I just want to know how long my probation will last," Rosa says. She hates the pleading tone that enters her voice. It's just that she's so nervous now. Nervous all the time. It's been over a week since she collided with the man in the three-piece suit. "I'm not even asking for it to be shortened. I just want to know how long it will last. It's eating away at me."

The secretary looks up. His eyes narrow. He's tanned, but it's a fake tan. He probably makes three times the amount Rosa does. And then Grammell makes ten times the amount the secretary makes. How many times is that what Rosa makes? She doesn't want to do the math. "Mr. Grammell is a very busy man, but, as I have already told you, I will relay your message to him. I'm sure I don't have to tell you that the best way to avoid this issue is to not end up on probation to begin with."

Rosa leaves, certain she will get no further, aware she might dig her hole deeper. As she walks out of the office, she looks around the halls she used to clean. Less crowded up here than in HR. She misses this silence, but the old woman's words about the voices come back to her. Rosa stops mid-step. She listens. Nothing. She goes closer to the gray wall, then puts her ear against it, the metal cold. She endures the discomfort. She listens again.

There is a deep, echoing sound, not unlike when she put a seashell to her ear the one time she went to the beach as a child. Beyond that, there is the sound of something moving. Liquid, maybe. Blood? Yes, she thinks. Blood. Blood moves through these walls, flowing freely. And behind the blood, voices. The same voices the old woman claimed to hear?

Rosa pulls away from the wall and rubs her temples. The stress is making her lose it. She wishes she could afford a psychiatrist. Anything to help numb the anxiety and paranoia. Anything at all.

———

ROSA IS dead tired whenever she returns to her apartment. Her days are tiring and her nights are filled with dreams of bloody floors in need of cleaning. She never had much of a relationship with her roommate, Valerie, but now she rarely has the energy to talk to her at all. On a Tuesday night, she manages to ask Valerie, "What would you do if I couldn't live here anymore?"

Valerie is watching TV while straightening her blond hair. "I'd probably ask Mark to move in, I guess. That should cover the rent." She doesn't look away from the television. Some comedians are doing a skit. Valerie does not laugh once.

Rosa stands in the doorway to her bedroom, her arms crossed. "Yeah, I guess that would work. Just worried about my job. Might not be there one day. I might not be able to afford rent." The words do not come easily.

"I'm sure it'll be fine," says Valerie. She adjusts the mirror on the table in front of her. "My hair looks straight, right?"

"Sure," says Rosa, but she's not really looking. She's thinking about messing up. She's thinking about what it's like to have to find a new job, how that's a job in itself, how Tyrius may not give her a good reference, how nobody pays much anymore, how she could lose her next job, too, and how that would be her third job loss in two years. Then she'd never find another position. Who would ever hire a thrice discarded cleaning woman? She'd be unemployable, and, in this world, unemployable means dead.

She tries to shake the thoughts away, telling herself it's all paranoia, telling herself it'll all work out.

———

THE STEEL FILE is the only piece of equipment that gets the mold out from under the bathroom sink. Rosa scrapes away, her arm hurting from the effort. How mold managed to grow in here, she'll never know, and she doesn't even want to think about how long she's missed it. She does know she'll end up getting the blame if anyone finds out about it.

Once the mold is gone, she scrubs the bottom of the sink, making certain there is no remnant. When done, she sprays disinfectant, not so much for the liquid itself but for the scent, which will hopefully mask any odor that came from the mold.

Rosa stands and washes her hands. She looks in the mirror. There are tears in her eyes. If she could miss mold, then what else could she miss? Enough to get her fired and start the process that would result in her being homeless. She knows that can happen. People like to think of the homeless as a different species, but Rosa has a cousin who became homeless. They never heard from him again. That could soon be her.

Unless, of course, she's off probation. She hasn't checked today. Perhaps she should wait until the end of her shift. The more time passes, the more likely she'll be off probation. So, why hurry to check now? Just wait until the end of the day. What time is it, anyway? 11:46 A.M. Work is over at 5:00. That's not long. She can go without checking it. Of course, she can always check it now and later. It's not going to make a difference. No need to be superstitious about it.

ON PROBATION.

Well, what did she expect?

She places her phone in her pocket. She places the file in it, too.

––––––

ON PROBATION. ON PROBATION. ON PROBATION. ON PROBATION. ON PROBATION.

––––––

It's 9:00 P.M. The subway is quiet. The file is heavy inside Rosa's pocket. She fell asleep in the break room after her shift ended. She hadn't meant to, just wanted to close her eyes for a few minutes before heading home, but, by the time she looked up, the clock read 8:45 P.M. She'd never been at Tyrius so late. She didn't turn around when walking down the halls, positive nothing good roamed the empty building. There could be something monstrous or there could simply be a person asking her why she's here so late, if she's up to something, if, maybe, she didn't belong here anymore.

Then, she thought of the dead and what they would ask her. Why not have a moral backbone? Why not feel pride at being discarded by such an institution?

And she will soon be discarded. She knows that now, no question about it. Be just like at her other job, like at any job. Once you're no longer useful you're gone. She's not sure why Grammell didn't just fire her instead of dragging it out with this probation. No doubt in a week or two they will sit her down and tell her it is not working out. That had to be the plan. The probation lingered, because they wanted her to trip up. They could even pat themselves on the back by saying they gave her a chance, didn't fire her after the initial incident with the client. Or perhaps they were all sadists here, enjoying watching her squirm.

The next infraction could be anything, too. Being late to work. Leaving a floor too wet. Leaving a floor too dry. Not catching a muddy footprint. Not making sure the bathrooms smell nice enough. Being seen too often. Not being seen often enough.

During the subway ride, she tries to recall a dream she had while she slept in the breakroom. She's positive she heard whispering, the voice telling her the only real way out, telling her a very good plan. Maybe that was the voice she was looking for when she put her ear to the wall.

When she arrives back home, she says to Valerie, "Remember us talking about a new roommate for you? You may need to look into it."

Valerie is on the couch, reading a magazine. "Yeah?" She sounds partially interested. "Found a new place?"

"Job problems," Rosa says, putting her coat away. She slips

the file out of her pants pocket and into the coat. "As in, I might not have one for much longer."

Valerie places the magazine down on her stomach. "Oh, that's terrible. Should look for a new one."

"Not a bad idea," Rosa says dryly. She goes to the refrigerator, takes out a yogurt, puts it back, and takes out a pint of ice cream. Mint chip. "Do you hate your job?"

"No, I love hairdressing," replies Valerie. "Do you hate yours?"

"Well, my job hates me," Rosa says. "I think it likes having me worried about when the other shoe will drop. I'm trying to get out of that cycle, though."

Valerie shrugs. "I say, just keep going even if you don't like it. Maybe look for something else better in the meantime and then quit if you get that."

"I think that's still the cycle," says Rosa. She starts eating her ice cream. It tastes great. No guilt and no anxiety at this moment, either. She now feels certain of her future, which brings with it a form of peace. "The only way out is probably dead. At least for people like us."

———

THERE ARE protestors outside of Tyrius Incorporated again. Rosa spots the old woman who grabbed her last time. She has a sign that reads GENOCIDE INCORPORATED. A couple of the protestors scream, "Enabler!" at Rosa as she goes through the doors of Tyrius.

She makes her way to the security check, placing her coat and pocketbook in the x-ray machine before walking through the scanner. "Good morning, Harry," she says to the security guard.

"Hey, Rosa," he replies, void of enthusiasm. He glances at

the screen that shows the result of the x-ray. "You have something in your coat?"

"A file," she says. There's not an ounce of concern in her voice. Nor in her, for that matter. "It's from here. I had it in my pocket and forgot to take it out when I went home the other day."

Harry says nothing for a moment. Rosa waits, her hands behind her back. "Well, I guess that's okay," Harry says. "You can go on through."

Rosa heads to the elevator. She places her hand in her coat pocket, feeling the file. It's cold. She steps into the elevator and selects the seventieth floor. Grammell's floor.

No one joins her, which is unusual but welcome. She leans against the side of the elevator, putting her ear to it. There is a rushing sound as the elevator ascends floor after floor. She tries to hear past the flow of blood, to hear into the very soul of the building. To hear the screams. They come. They deafen her initially, but the screams turn to words of gratitude, telling Rosa she's doing the right thing after doing the wrong thing for too long a while. One or two of them ask what took her so long, their tone full of haunting rage. Why did it take all this for her to realize what system she existed in?

The doors open. The hall is quiet. She walks down it and, despite still hearing the words of Tyrius' victims and the flow of blood, she's confident. More confident than she has been in her entire life. It's refreshing, and she knows life will be unlivable if she ever has to go back to how it was before she decided to be free.

She turns into the office of Grammell's secretary. He looks up and sighs. "He's not in, just like last time," he says to her. He looks more tired than before. It's his eyes. There seem to be more wrinkles around them. She wonders how she looks through his eyes. He likely thinks her ugly, within and without.

"He was almost always in his office when I was working up here," she says. She points at the closed door that leads to Grammell's room. "I bet you he's in there right now."

"That's it," says the secretary. "I'm calling security. I've had enough of you harassing me."

That won't do. She needs to see Grammell. He's the heart of the problem. The voices of the dead said so.

Rosa removes the file from her coat and stabs the secretary in the eye. The file breaks through his glasses and goes into his brain. She grabs the back of his head, forcing the file deeper into him. He lets out a sound that is unlike anything Rosa heard before: a mix of a shriek and a sob that ends as quickly as it started. Rosa lets go and watches as the secretary wobbles in his chair; she wonders what areas of the brain the file cut through. It's hard for her to fully accept she stabbed him.

Eventually, the secretary falls forward. Rosa removes the file. There is a squishing sound as she takes it out of the dead man's skull. After a moment's consideration about what she has now become, Rosa tries the door to Grammell's office. It's unlocked.

He's not inside. Misery washes over her. The secretary wasn't lying. "This is horrible," she whispers. She drops the file on the ground and sits behind Grammell's desk. She wipes the blood on her hands over his keyboard. She waits for the voices of Tyrius' victims to guide her. She wonders if she should kill herself. She knows that she's not getting out of this building alive. A place like this will not allow it.

And then he's there, in the doorway, staring at her. "You did this?" he asks, his voice hoarse.

Rosa makes a gun with her fingers and points at Grammell. "Bang," she says. "Bang. Bang. Bang."

SEVENTEEN WEEKS AGO, Jonathan Grammell sat across from Rosa in his office. He wore a black suit that day with a brightly colored tie, which made Rosa think he must be a warm person despite the clinical atmosphere in the building. "So, you're going to be cleaning my office," he said. "I don't usually use this office to see guests, so it's likely the two people most often in here will be you and me. Figured I'd want to meet you in that case."

Rosa was not sure what to say. She went with, "I'll clean it as if it was my own home."

"Maybe that's good," he said, smirking. "But maybe I should go and see how clean your home is before officially hiring you, right?"

She laughed, not sure if he was making fun of her.

TURN-AROUND

TY ZINK

It's been four days since I fired Sam Walton. There's nothing particularly significant about that. If it were three days since, or seven, or thirteen, that would mean something. Those numbers hold weight. Nobody cares about the number four. But four days is how long Sam's been haunting me. So I suppose if someone should care about that, it's me.

The day after I fired him, he was hanging out in the gas station across the street from the office. I crossed the lot to grab my usual—two shrink-wrapped breakfast burritos—and I saw him sitting in a booth by the window. Eating two breakfast burritos, funnily enough. And he saw me. I'm pretty sure I saw his eyes tracking me, anyway, though his head never turned. But when I walked in the convenience store, Sam was gone before the door jingle faded. Not even a wrapper left on the table. I got my breakfast and walked out. But as I was nearly to the street that separated me from my office, call it instinct, call it fate—I had no reason to, but I looked back toward the convenience store.

There he was, hands pressed against the glass of the door. Watching me.

Haunting is too strong a word. Stalking, that's more accurate.

He's vindicating me, really. I had my doubts about letting him go. But after this? No, I made the right call.

Sam was a hard worker. He was always ready to take on additional assignments, work extra hours without expecting overtime, and he delivered results. In many ways, he was the model employee. But he wasn't a good culture fit. The women felt strange about him. The men felt even worse. He had those queer mannerisms, after all. Everyone knows one, whether they'd like to or not. Always too open, too friendly, too... something. A certain *je ne sais quoi*, as Sam himself would've put it. He was always using flowery language like that. Figures.

I can see him from the third-floor break room window. Even from here, he looks a total mess. Disheveled hair sticks up on one side of his head. His suit is wrinkled, as if he has been sleeping in it. The dark rings under his eyes are visible even here. He's looked like this every day since I fired him.

———

"HERE'S MY ADVICE: go easy on the guy. If he goes home and ends up hanging by his necktie, the last thing you need is being kept up at night knowing that's on you."

John's facial expression is casual, his voice conversational. I'm not the first manager he's given this advice to, that much is clear, and I won't be the last. He's possibly said this line underneath this very overhang to every one of those other managers. What's not clear is whether this worst-case scenario is purely hypothetical or personal experience. He lights his cigarette with a wrinkled but steady hand. He glances over and offers me the lighter.

I choose to believe he's exaggerating.

"So what do I tell him?" I ask. "He's going to want to know why."

"Just remember the three magic words," John says. "At. Will. Employment."

I rub my temple and sigh. "Still, I'd like to have *some* excuse. There's nothing."

"Nothing? Walton hasn't made a single mistake ever?"

"No performance problems. Doesn't give managers problems. No harassment allegations. And I can't exactly put 'he creeps me out' in his personnel file."

"Come on. Not a single gripe?"

"Well. He's a bit of a perfectionist," I say, and an idea hits me. "And he takes a bit longer than the rest of the team to complete his reports. Never late, and they're excellently compiled when he does get them to me. But his output falls behind the others for it."

John claps my shoulder, and I nearly drop my cigarette. "There we go!" he says. "We'll make a manager outta you in no time!" My eyebrow raises, and he notices. "What I mean is that you can't think too hard about Walton—he's good, but he's got a line of other qualified guys who want his spot, and *your* job is to make sure you fill that spot with the right one. And ideally, it's not a guy who'll grope anyone he's left alone in the restroom with."

"Sam's never done that."

"Like you said. No harassment complaints, *yet*. But you know his type." John takes a long drag. Smoke fills the space between us. "You gonna wait around until you get a complaint, or are you gonna be proactive about it?"

I snuff my cigarette out on the brick wall of our office building. "Thanks, John," I say as I slide my key-card against the door scanner. I hear a murmured "Mm-hmm" in response as the door beeps and the lock clicks.

———

"Ultimately, this is about your turn-around time."

Sam looks in near-tears. "My... my turn-around time?" he chokes out.

"Yes," I reply. "You've failed to meet our expectations for processed reports this month. We brought this up in your last evaluation, if you recall. Since we've had no signs of improvement in the time we've given you... well. We can't hold you to lighter standards than the rest of the team, can we?"

That's bullshit. I've never talked to him about this prior to this meeting. I just hope I said it smooth enough that he doesn't question it.

"I... I see," Sam says. He stares down at his hands folded in his lap, bites his lip. Those little mannerisms that made the other men in my unit nervous. Anyway, he seems to have bought it.

"I'm very sorry, Sam. But I wish you luck in your further endeavors. Perhaps a less competitive workplace would be a better fit."

"S-sure. One where my—" he gulps. "My turn-around... doesn't..." This timidness is so off-putting. I wish he wouldn't wear his heart on his sleeve like that.

In as even a tone as I can muster, I say, "Denise is grabbing your affects from your desk. Once she brings them, you're free to go."

Sam pushes his chair back and nearly stumbles in an effort to stand. "N-no, I'll ju—" and he falters a bit. I hear him murmur softly, "T-turn around." And he does, toward the door.

I step up and away from my desk toward him. "Are you sure? Listen, if you apply somewhere else, we'll be happy to give you a recommend—"

The door snaps shut behind him.

———

EVERY DAY SINCE, I've seen him hanging around the office. The gas station first. On day two, he was there underneath the overhang, the favored smoking spot. Who knows how long he was waiting, looking through the door. I went to the restroom instead, and crossed my fingers nobody noticed the smoke billowing out the window. I couldn't help glancing out to the sidewalk below. Not that I could even see the overhang from there; I just had that sneaking suspicion that he was still lurking there.

Yesterday, he managed to find my office window, despite it being on the third floor, and spent the whole day looking up at it from the parking lot. About 10:00 AM, I pushed my desk toward the door so he couldn't see the back of my head anymore. He was gone once I clocked out for the day, but when I checked at about a quarter 'til 5:00, he was there. Watching. Even now, I'm in the break room, and he's managed to figure out where I'm at again.

The thing is, it's about 11:15 PM now. I haven't left the office today.

Neither has Sam.

He's positioned himself in the perfect spot in the parking lot below that he'd be staring at me should I look out. At least, I assume he's giving me the same blank stare he's been giving me for half a week. I can't make out his expression in the shadow cast by the parking lot lamp post. But if he's going through the effort of stalking me, he could at least look like he's going to murder me. No, scratch that, forget I even

131

thought about it. My nose is nearly against the glass now. But I still can't make out anything of him.

The phone rings.

I jump at the sudden noise, and I nearly lose grip on my coffee cup. The mug is saved, barely, though the now mercifully lukewarm liquid is a dark stain across my white shirt. I stumble over to the break room sink and yank at the paper towel roll, but my shaky hands only pull off scraps. I blame it on drinking coffee when it's nearly midnight. Who the hell is calling the office this late anyw—oh. Of course.

Despite myself, I reach over to the break room phone and pick up.

I get nothing but a dial tone for my trouble.

I sigh, and hang up the phone. I'm not even halfway back toward the sink when it rings again. Against my better judgment, I give it one more shot.

"Sam? If this is you, I swear I will call the pol—"

"*Turn around*," a small, soft voice comes through the phone speaker.

"W-what?" I ask. But I'm met with silence. Reluctantly, I do as he asks. I lower the phone and look back, and I'm facing the window again. The same one he's staring at right now.

I take a step.

Another.

Another.

And I'm looking out into the parking lot. Dark as it is, I see my face clearly in the glass. I try to stall my quivering lip, narrow my widened eyes. Make myself look presentable. I don't see Sam anymore. But I hear his voice. Much firmer this time. Louder. This isn't coming from the phone.

"*Turn around.*"

There are two faces reflected in the window. I still look like a mess. Sam looks even worse.

Same blank stare. But where his hair is sticking up, I see a dark spot. It's dripping.

He reaches out and grabs both sides of my face. His palms put so much pressure against my ears that my skull might pop. Cold fingertips dig into the corners of my eyes.

In the darkened window, I see a grin cross Sam's face.

"TURN AROUND."

RETURN POLICY

DUSTIN WALKER

I parked the van across from one of those ultra-posh playgrounds, where all the equipment is made with bright-colored plastic and the artificial turf is so soft Junior could fall from 20 feet up and not get a bruise. The place buzzed with laughing kids, which made me feel even shittier about my job.

After hauling my ReGen-issued duffel bag out of the back, I chugged the rest of my Mountain Dew and hoped it'd help with the hangover. It didn't. Then I headed up the manicured walkway of 4526 Bayview Drive and gave myself the usual mental pep talk:

Remember, every return is an opportunity for education. A chance to grow the resistance.

I sucked in one last breath, patted the speaking notes in my shirt pocket to make sure they were still there, and then knocked. It took a minute or so before I finally heard movement from behind the door. A short man in thick-framed glasses answered. I assumed he was David Cobb, the dad, so I jumped right into the script.

"Hello there, my name's Rick. I'm with the Returns

Department at ReGen." I spoke softly and tried to sound warm and understanding. "I'm here for Angela."

"Come in, please," said David.

He led me through a foyer bigger than my studio apartment and into their living room. The place smelled of flowers and hairspray. Gleaming-white furniture and floor-to-ceiling windows made the room uncomfortably bright.

A woman sat on the sofa, knitting. She didn't look at me, just kept staring at a blank TV screen.

"Honey, Rick here is from ReGen," David said. She must have been his wife, Wendy Cobb.

"Wonderful," she replied in a distant voice. Her fingers twiddled the needles, winding through a tangled mass of wool that piled on her lap.

I'd focus on David after processing the return, I thought, since Wendy still seemed in shock.

"I'm very sorry for your loss. I know this is difficult for both of you."

David looked at the floor. "We didn't think it would be like this. Her body just fell apart so quickly."

His word choice surprised me. Parents never usually mentioned details like that, but I supposed everyone processes grief differently.

"Where is Angela now?"

"Upstairs in her room, third door on the right." He glanced over at his wife and sighed. "Could you meet us in the kitchen afterwards? We'd prefer not to see her being removed."

"Yes, of course."

I headed upstairs, my duffle bag banging against each thick-carpeted step. The sick-sweet stench of rot gradually pushed away all those bright, flowery smells as I climbed higher. Flies pinged against the hallway light. Dark splotches stained the rug.

I stopped in front of Angela's room and listened for any trace of movement. Nothing. Just the muted laughter of kids playing in that posh playground across the street.

I put down my bag and pulled out my supplies: polypropylene overalls, an N95 mask, and long yellow gloves. Some guys who process returns like to suit up in the van, but not me. When you arrive at their door like you're about to haul away a pile of toxic trash, it makes the whole process feel too clinical. Too inhuman. The least we could do is show these folks some compassion.

The kind of compassion John showed my wife and I when he came for Rory.

As I pulled on the gloves and zipped up my suit, my mind drifted back to the day we first met John. The way he looked at us with those sorrow-filled eyes while my wife and I hugged each other and cried. How he put a hand on my shoulder and told me this wasn't our fault. He explained that ReGen had a system for preying on grieving parents like us and that thousands of people across the country had also fallen for their sales pitch. Parents who would do anything—pay anything—for just a chance to hold their children again.

But most importantly, John convinced me to join him in recruiting other grieving parents to help fight ReGen's growing popularity in the U.S.

So I quit my job as an electrician and went to work for the very company that caused me so much pain. Sure, I processed returns for ReGen. But that was just a way to get close to the families at the right time. I followed John's lead by offering the parents counselling, a much-needed hug, and a bit of empathy from someone who had been in their shoes.

Most of all, I educated them about ReGen's return policy. I advised them never to sign the non-disclosure agreement that would arrive in the mail the next day. Because if they did, they wouldn't be able to tell the media or anyone else about what happened to their children.

In other words, they'd be powerless to warn others about all the empty promises ReGen makes.

Some parents joined us, but most didn't. Because when you're in that state of mind—so emotionally drained that your legs feel like cotton—you'll sign almost anything with a bit of coaxing. The promise of paying for a long-overdue funeral often does the trick.

Fully dressed, I pulled a high-voltage Taser from my bag. Nervous sweat made my skin hot and slimy beneath the plastic suit; my stomach curdled with caffeine and anxiety.

I turned the knob and slowly pushed Angela's door open.

Sunshine filtered through the twisted Venetian blinds, scattering just enough light to make out torn posters clinging to the walls. I flicked on the light switch. Books and shattered glass littered the floor. A plywood desk sat overturned in the corner.

Angela lay on her bed, staring at the ceiling, her gaunt skin a marbled patchwork of dull greens and pale yellows. She wore a tattered dress and held a stuffed unicorn to her chest.

At first, I thought she couldn't move—a lot of them end up immobile near the end. But as soon as I stepped inside her room, she sat up in slow jerking movements. Dead skin peeled away from her arms and back, clinging to the bed like gum stuck between the pages of a book. She turned toward me with empty sockets, and I wondered what color her eyes had been.

Even after processing dozens of returns, these types of scenes never leave me. They sit inside my mind, deep and visceral, kicking up flashbacks of Rory's final reanimated days. The ones where he sat limp in the corner of his room, slamming the back of his head rhythmically against the wall for hours. Or when he smashed through the patio door, eviscerating himself on the shards of glass.

And whenever those moments flooded back to me, I questioned whether being neck deep in this shit was worth it. Whether enticing the odd parent to speak to the media was really making an impact, really helping the resistance.

Or if I'm just playing the sucker again by punching a clock for the company that made my suffering so much worse.

I sparked the Taser to make sure it was on.

She stared at me, her face blank yet indescribably sad. The kind of sorrow that maybe only the dead can understand. Angela raised a shaking, skeletal arm and pointed behind me.

I turned around.

Words were scrawled in blood above the door:
WHEN WILL I GET TO COME BACK AGAIN?

I stared at it like an idiot for a few seconds before it finally sank in.

Fuck, she knows. She knows why I'm here.

I gawked at the writing for a minute more, wondering what to do next. They don't usually understand what's happening at this stage because their brains are so decomposed. But Angela seemed lucid and entirely aware of what was happening to her.

I turned back around and flinched: she stood right in front of me, her tiny face inches from my chest. Her empty eyes staring up into my own.

My muscles filled with concrete. Neither of us moved.

What is she trying to do? Does she want something from me?

I watched her a while longer, unsure how to react, before finally mustering the courage to speak.

"Angela? Can you hear me?"

She tilted her head to the side, as if trying to process my words, and then moved toward me.

I stumbled backwards. She stopped and looked at me with that tilted-head gaze of hers again.

My stomach tightened and my mouth went dry. I wondered if she was trying to say something. To tell me she was hurting, maybe, or that she didn't want to leave.

She lunged forward with her arms out.

I thrust the Taser into her abdomen on instinct.

Angela stiffened as electric clatter filled the room. She tumbled onto the floor, still as stone.

I dropped the Taser, hands shaking. Normally, I didn't feel much of anything when I stunned them. They were just empty husks by the time the parents requested a return, incapable of any thoughts or emotion. But with Angela, it felt like I had killed her.

Did her parents know she could still hear? Did they realize a piece of her still suffered inside that rotting shell? That she was still aware of everything going on?

I forced the questions out of my head. It didn't matter now. Angela had passed on and her parents were waiting for me downstairs.

I placed her slick remains in a body bag, picked her up, and carried her out of the room. I always tried to be careful and respectful when I brought them out, holding them like sleeping children. Which, in a way, they were. But I was even more careful with Angela as I stepped cautiously down each stair.

After placing the girl's body in the van, I slipped off my gloves and mask and went back to the house with my clip-board. I struggled about whether to mention Angela's condition to David and Wendy. Considering they were probably still in shock, I couldn't imagine they knew Angela was even remotely lucid. And telling them this might make their lives even more unbearable.

It took me a couple of minutes to find the kitchen, which shined just as unnaturally bright as their living room. I had never been in a place with so much white tile and stainless steel before. David and Wendy sat at a small table next to a window overlooking their backyard. Wendy still knitted at the same steady pace as before, her tangled mess of wool now swollen to twice its original size.

"Are we all set?" David asked, not making eye contact.

I hesitated, not sure how to play this. "All set, yeah."

He looked at me. "Did she try to hug you?"

My body froze. *He knew. He knew the entire time she was still in there.*

I nodded, too caught off guard to say anything.

"Yeah, Angela's a big hugger. Always has been, even with strangers," David said, his face bending into a faint smile. "I'm just glad you came to finally get her out of there."

"Get her out?" I dropped the clipboard and my fists tightened. "You say that like she's a piece of garbage?"

"David, they don't always tell these people about Eternal," Wendy said, putting down her knitting. "They're only sub-contractors, I think, or something like that."

David's mouth popped open. "Oh, shit. You probably think I'm a monster." He got up and grabbed a pamphlet off the kitchen counter with ReGen's infinity-sign logo on it. He handed it to me. "Sorry, I thought you knew. We're beta-testers for the new Eternal Program."

The glossy pamphlet showed a smiling elderly couple having dinner with a pre-teen boy. In giant letters were the words: *Now you never have to say goodbye.*

"The technology is remarkable." His face brightened. "I don't completely understand the physics behind it, but her 'essence,' as they call it, is transferred from her old body—the one you removed for us—to her new body, which is in a room downstairs right now. It's like her very soul is getting ready to start a new life."

"It's not her soul." Wendy's voice took on the texture of sandpaper. "Angela's consciousness is being transferred from one reinforced membrane to another via a high-speed Wi-Fi-based signal. And in about an hour, her *mind* will exist in another child's body."

"Wow, Wendy. Leave it to you to make even our child's everlasting spirit sound like something cold and sterile."

"I'm not getting into this in front of... him." She nodded toward me, like I'm a waiter who had overstayed his welcome at the table.

They continued to bicker as I scanned the pamphlet. It said the Eternal Program provided users with up to five "hosts" per year that could receive the consciousness of a "recently passed" child.

For a second, I thought this might work for Rory. And just the remote possibility of speaking to him again warmed a dark and empty place inside of me. But even if I could somehow cover the $675,000 price tag, the Eternal program wasn't made for people like me.

It had to be set up in advance—like an insurance policy—so that the child's "essence" could immediately transfer into a host once he or she died. If the transfer didn't start right away, or if it was interrupted before completion, the person would be lost for good.

"Excuse me? Hello?" Wendy waved her hands at me. "Do you need us to sign something or... ?"

I picked up the clipboard and handed it to her.

Questions banged through my head as she scrawled her unnecessarily flamboyant signature on the dotted lines.

How many parents are taking part in the Eternal Program? Where did ReGen get all the so-called hosts?

"Here you go." She thrust the clipboard at me. Her eyes

narrowed and a thin smile creased her mascara-plastered face. I recognized that look. I used to get it all the time from homeowners when doing electrical work in gated communities. It was rich-people speak for "get the fuck out."

I grit my teeth, holding back the urge to unleash a tirade on the couple. Judging by the worried looks on their faces, they knew I was pissed. But I doubt they understood why.

For most people, a visit from the Returns Department marks the second-darkest time in their lives. A moment when their bad decisions become achingly clear. They feel like fools, and life once again seems hopeless and unfair.

But for David and Wendy, my visit hardly meant anything at all. Their daughter would be back soon. And unlike the poor bastards like me who grabbed onto that thin sliver of hope, the Cobbs really would experience all the things ReGen promised.

Right after I hauled away their garbage.

I left without saying a word and stomped back to the van. I wrapped my fingers around the door handle and was about to yank it open when I caught sight of a Mercedes pulling up to the park. A black-haired boy jumped out—he was six or seven, roughly Rory's age—and sprinted toward a chrome teeter-totter shaped like a rocket ship.

He played on it for a few minutes, then ran over to the swings. Met up with another boy. Ran around the swings again.

I started to picture Rory on that playground, but stopped myself. Imagining him at that sparkling park for spoiled brats wouldn't be doing my boy justice. He never played at places like that. Hell, he'd probably laugh at that fucking stupid rocket ship teeter-totter.

So instead, I pictured David. How tomorrow he'd be smiling contentedly while watching his daughter—in her new body—run around the park. Maybe Wendy would come out and bring them some lemonade or Perrier or whatever rich fucks drank on a summer day.

I gripped the door handle so hard my knuckles turned white. Hot lead bubbled inside me.

The more I thought about David Cobb—his face curved into an undeserving smile—the more that posh playground looked different to me. Like an oily shadow had settled on it, saturating everything and reminding me that I'd never get to play with my kid again. Not there or anywhere else.

I spun around and walked back to the Cobbs' house.

It took me just seconds to find their electrical meter. Just minutes to smash its protective plastic covering with a paving stone and pry the entire unit from the wall.

With their power and Wi-Fi cut, I went back to my van and waited. I don't remember how long it took, but I heard Wendy scream first. Her shrill voice like knitting needles dragging along the hood of the van.

I headed back up the manicured walkway of 4526 Bayview Drive and gave myself the usual mental pep talk:

Remember, every return is an opportunity for education. A chance to grow the resistance.

I sucked in one last breath, patted the speaking notes in my shirt pocket to make sure they were still there, and then knocked.

John would be proud.

EMPTY

NOAH LEMELSON

The order started innocently enough. A middle-aged woman with dyed-gold hair and three kids, two girls, one boy, the latter of whom was complaining loudly that he 'wanted ice cream instead!' We got that a lot.

"Welcome to Frozen Yoggie's House of Yogurt," I said with my plastic smile. "Would you like a sample of—"

"Yeah, we've been to one of these before," the woman said. "Give me three large Birthday Cake cups. It's her birthday." She pointed to the young girl beside her, pink dress and crown, mouth squeezed against the chilled glass that protected our two-dozen varieties of toppings.

"Three Birthday Cakes, coming up," I said, turning round, past my manager Jane, languidly flipping the pages of a Rolling Stones, and Dennis, swinging his mop against the indomitable stain that half-hid beneath the sink. My eyes swept from flavor to flavor, near forty in all, from "French Roast" to "Pumped-Up Pumpernickel" to the massively unpopular "Yogurt-Flavored" frozen yogurt.

My breath stopped when I noticed the red light blinking.

Empty. I looked down and read *Birthday Cake*, then glanced up again and down, trying to convince myself I had somehow misread the sign, or that I had gone temporarily colorblind, or that I was mad, anything rather than the truth that we were out of Birthday Cake frozen yogurt.

"You sure you wouldn't prefer Crazy Cotton Candy?" I asked swiftly, Jane glancing up to stare as I stammered my excuses. "Or Bittersweet Butterscotch? There are so many flavors to choose from, why don't you taste a few?"

"I said, *it's her birthday!*" The woman glared at me, nose flaring, as she pointed down at the child, who had moved on to licking the glass and making cat noises.

"Leah!" Jane shouted, "There's a refill carton in the storeroom. Stop wasting time."

I gritted my teeth, glancing at Denis, who wouldn't return my look, then at our intern Claire, who stared dead-eyed by the cash register. Poor girl, it was clear she still hadn't gotten over our last trip in. And she had been so close to Charles.

"Wouldn't it make more sense if we wait until we need to refill several of the machines before going into storage?" I offered, with empty hope.

Jane rolled her eyes and tossed her magazine to the ground. "We can't live in fear. It's inefficient, and unfair to our customers. In these trying times people need access to their favorite frozen desserts more than ever, and if you're not willing to occasionally risk your life to provide them, then you should never have gotten into the service industry."

The threat was there and not subtle. I had worked hard for my thirteen an hour. It paid for two trips to the food court a day, and sometimes left me with enough discretionary cash to pay for my yearly doctor's appointment. Before things had gotten crazy, I was even on a path to promotion, into the management track, might have even saved enough to move out of my mother's apartment. But then the infestation started spreading, and we lost our old manager. Corporate got all spooked because of the stock market and everything just kind of went to shit. I sucked in my growing panic and clenched my eyes.

"It's fine," Jane said, with more than a little irritation. "We need someone watching the cash register anyhow. Denis, Clair, suit up!"

Clair. The blood drained from the young woman's face, her finger tapping the edge of the register as she tried to find a way to say "no," to create an excuse, true or fabricated, something, but she just breathlessly stammered. I willed her on, the poor girl. She had been interning here for the past two years. How was it fair for her to die in my stead?

"Yes..." she said finally, her voice weak, "I'll—"

"I'll go," I interrupted. "Clair needs more customer experience, and I'm a better shot anyhow."

"Fine," Jane said, unlocking the gun rack that hung by the cup dispenser.

"Ahem," the golden-haired woman said.

"Our apologies Ma'am, we'll have it out in a minute," shouted Jane as she loaded her M16. The customer snorted and muttered something rude about 'the millennial work ethic.' Denis silently unhooked the dolly, a pistol in his free hand. As for myself, I took a flare gun, since the experts said they feared light, and a sawed-off shotgun, since the experts were often wrong.

We gathered by the door, checking our uniforms' built-in flashlights as Jane typed in the security code. "The Birthday Cake refill should be in the back freezer. Remember to check corners; the bastard likes to skulk and jump." I tried to control my panic. This wasn't unusual, not anymore. Nearly every store had one or two, it was just part of the job description. Hell, as our corporate spokesman had pointed out in our last training, most employees could expect to make it through their whole career with little more than a few flesh wounds and scars.

I heard whispering. It was Denis, he was speaking in some language, I'm not sure what, probably his native tongue. I never talked much to Denis, nor he to me. It wasn't smart to get too attached to co-workers, so I never really figured out where he was from or what his original name was before he anglicized it. As the pressure locks released, I had a sudden urge to ask, to know the man, to understand the meanings of his melodic whispers. I could only guess, but they sounded like prayers.

"Clair, lock the door behind us, let's move!" shouted Jane.

The darkness hit us as soon as the door slid shut, near complete besides the glare of our flashlights, which were insufficient to cover even a tenth of the gaping storeroom. The smell rolled over us soon after, a subtler strike of pungent rot that covered even the sickly sugary smell of frozen yogurt. We stood still, sweeping out lights around the crates and rusted forklifts. Cardboard boxes lay trampled, soaked by a leaking gasoline barrel that had been shredded during our last trip in, leaving a shimmering pond of black. I'm not sure if we were taking a moment to tactically assess the situation, or if we were just collectively hesitant to move. Charles's screams still echoed in my memory.

"In the back freezer," Jane repeated in a whisper, perhaps to herself.

I took out my flare gun and fired into the center of the room. It flew in an arc, and with it a wave of red rolled through the room. I could have sworn I saw the creature three times over, its grotesque face illuminated in a far corner, its elongated arms draped over gasoline barrels or trampled trash bins.

With trepidation we moved forward, carefully checking every angle. *'Have an eye in all directions. Assume it's in every possible hiding spot. Lose your focus and you lose your head.'* I silently repeated the advice we had been given during our eight-hour training and team building sessions last year. At least we got those; so many companies didn't even bother with safety training until they got hit with a lawsuit, and even then just posted a few video courses online. It was nice to think that Frozen Yoggie's cared about us.

We made slow progress. Yet there was no movement among the shadows, no strange chittering whispers or the scuttling of a thousand synchronized legs. It was almost like normal times, except for dried husks of egg clutches on the wall and the cracked, chewed bones of Charles by our feet.

Where was the monster? I turned to light up the back corner, where a labyrinth of cardboard boxes and file cabinets sat, mostly old tax forms and other paperwork, dull and dense. A perfect place for the beast to hide.

"Remember, goal's get in and get out, don't bother trying to go for a kill shot," Jane said. It was possible to kill the creatures, difficult, but possible. I had seen videos on YouTube, but corporate downplayed them. The monsters were territorial and mated faster than rabbits on Viagra; you kill one and another would take its place within hours, sometimes minutes. Maybe if there had been a coordinated response when the infestation had started, but what would have been the point? Someone would have slacked, and then we'd be here anyway.

"Got any flashbangs?" I asked.

Jane shook her head. "Still on backorder. Corporate says we need to ration. Honestly I don't want to badger them. A shop in Greenwood got closed 'cause they were wasting too much flamethrower fuel on egg catches. We can't be profligate."

I never intended to work here so long. This job was meant to be a stepping stone, just a way to pay off some student loans until I tried for grad school. It's not like my anthropology degree was doing me any good in the meanwhile. How fun it was to try and tease out why we are the way we are, to push society under the microscope, to craft grand, distant theories in the comfort of a classroom or within that 54-page white tower that was my thesis. What wasted time! Things are the way they are because that's how they are and it didn't matter the theoretical framework or model. The reasons can't matter, because even if they did, you couldn't do shit about it. No one outside of my professors would ever read my thesis, but there was a woman waiting who still wanted some frozen yogurt.

"Here we are," said Jane. Denis whispered something and made a sign with his hands as I swung my light over the massive freezers. *Choco-blast... California Caramel... Blueberry Swirl... Birthday Cake!* I turned the hatch and it clanked open, frozen winds buffeting me. Behind stood mountains of fogged plastic canisters, the multicolored swirls of the Birthday Cake yogurt clear to see within. Hundreds of plastic boxes, thousands, designed to last centuries if need be. I picked up the closest and hauled it over to the dolly.

"Maybe it's sleeping," Jane said. "We got lucky."

"Lucky," I repeated, wrapping the chains around the canister. Couldn't risk losing it 'cause of a crack in the floor.

"Actually, our Caramel supplies are on yellow," Jane said. "Denis, open up that California locker."

Denis nodded and walked over. The hatch had frozen over stiff, so it took a good minute of groaning before he was able to make any progress. I waited, nerves on end, while Jane scanned round, her M16 at the ready.

"What you planning on doing with your vacation days?" she asked suddenly.

"Oh, uh," I stammered. It's not like I had many, and I usually saved what I had in case I got maimed and needed a week off to convalesce. "I guess I'll do some Uber driving or something."

"Nice," Jane said. "Good and relaxing. It's important to rest sometimes. The job can take a lot out of you."

"Sure," I said.

"It's not what you do when things are easy that makes you who you are," she said. "It's what you do when things get hard. That's what I think."

"Yeah," I said. Jane had never talked to me like this before, hadn't really talked to me much at all besides terse instructions and passive-aggressive feedback. Perhaps there was something about the darkness around us, something about being there, in the lair of the beast, knowing that your life could be snatched from you at any minute by a dozen bladed hands, that made you want to look to your coworkers and remind them that you are human, that they are human, that despite everything, we had that in common. Or maybe she just wanted to fill the silence.

"There!" Denis said, the door creaking in agreement. He pulled it open and—

His scream was sudden and short. We twirled round to see a shape lunge from the inside, as swift as a mousetrap. One moment Denis was there, the next he was dead. Long and twisting, like a millipede, hundreds of long arms with too many fingers, each a blade, the monster tore into Denis's body, a frenzied feast, teeth gnashing, hair matted and torn.

"Fire!" Jane shouted, letting loose a round. The muzzle flashed like a strobe light, the monster turning from its meal of our coworker and swerving round with preternatural speed and agility.

I fumbled with my sawed-off as the creature reared up. It stared down at me with its hungry eyes, it lips red and curled into a smile. Droplets of Denis's viscera fell upon me, but I was disturbed more than anything by how closely the beast's face resembled a man's. Two eyes, a nose in the right place, ears small and round. If it were decapitated, could I tell the difference between this monster's head and that of some random neighbor or acquaintance? If not for its insectoid body, it could hide among us, spreading its eggs in public, no one the wiser. Scientists had explained the similarity. It was no mystery, apparently, or so I had read from a headline on Facebook. I didn't check out the article to discover the details, who has time for that?

The monster screeched, I fired.

"Nice shot!" Jane shouted as the beast fell back, but I knew it was no kill. I tossed my shotgun on the floor and started to push forward the dolly as fast as I could manage. Jane ran backwards, covering our retreat with a burst of bullets as the monster regained its bearings and started to scuttle along the wall.

I gripped my flare gun and blindfired behind me. Only one shot left. The creature screeched at the sudden burst of light. I glanced back to see that Jane had managed a few clean shots on the beast, but nothing that would keep it down.

I slammed the trolley into the door and started to bang with my fist.

"Clair! Clair! Open up now!" I shouted. Jane kept firing as the beast circled round, dodging this way and that, knocking over a stack of crates and smashing through barrels. I ran over to the control panel and clicked in the passcode. The light beeped red.

"Clair!" I shouted.

"I'm trying!" I heard her voice muffled through the steel. "It won't open! Some error!"

I glanced up and froze. "Shit." Jane turned round and

made a similar expletive. The hydraulics that controlled the door had been torn into, ripped to utter pieces. The monster, it knew what it was doing, had lured us to the deepest part of its nest and cut off the exit.

"The manual crank!" Jane shouted. "Clair, turn it! Now!"

The door started to creak open, slowly, inch by agonizing inch. The monster was getting closer, in swerving lunges back and forth, as Jane peppered shots.

"How many rounds?" I asked, aiming my last flare.

"Not many," Jane replied through grit teeth. We didn't have ammo, we didn't have time. The beast was closing in far faster than the door was opening.

I was going to die here, I realized. I was going to die trying to deliver three cups of "Birthday Cake" flavored frozen yogurt. I searched through my life, trying to figure out where I went wrong, what decisions of mine led to this. Despite my efforts, I could come to no conclusion other than that my fate was inevitable, that I would have ended up here sooner or later no matter what I'd tried.

The monster splashed through the puddle of gasoline on the floor, before leaping onto the wall again. Jane sucked in her breath suddenly.

"I was going to recommend you for promotion," she said.

"You did?" I asked.

"Well, I didn't get around to it, but I was thinking about recommending you," she said, firing off another round. "You know how it is."

I nodded.

"You work hard," she said. "You give the customers what they want, no matter the cost. You're a good woman, Leah."

With that she grabbed the flare gun from my hand. Before I could say anything she was running forward, jumping into the puddle of gasoline. The monster turned and screeched, lunging at Jane. She fired downwards. A burst of flame roared up, engulfing both her and the beast, as their screams harmonized in the suddenly burning pyre.

The door finally flung open, Clair panting on the other side. I pushed the trolley through, then jumped forward, cranking the door shut, the sounds of burning agony muffling as it slammed.

"Denis? Jane?" Clair asked with a pale face.

I shook my head and pointed towards the canister of frozen yogurt. "Get it loaded, we have a customer waiting."

"Yes you do!" came the voice of the golden-haired woman. "We've been waiting for nearly ten minutes!" The kids were clearly bored. One was taking a nap on the floor while the other two were taking paper cups from our drink machine and tossing them at one another.

"My sincere apologies, my associate is getting those right away." I said, panting. I tried to clean myself up as best I could in the moment, wiping off Denis's blood, and knocking the ashes from my uniform. I couldn't take the time to calm myself or wash up fully. I was still on the clock, which meant any emotions or trauma needed to be pushed down, to be processed on my own time. I had a job to do, and Jane didn't die so that I could do that job poorly. I stared at the golden-haired woman and smiled. "Can I offer you a free frozen yogurt for your troubles?"

The woman snorted. "Our entire order should be free! Where do people get off these days? Expect a pat on the back for barely doing their job… But yes, I would like a Caramel. Extra-Large. With pecans!"

"Of course. Thank you so much for your patience." I walked over to the yogurt machine, my muscles aching and vision blurry. Jane had almost recommended me. I was so close, again. I must be doing something right.

I pulled out a large cup and placed it under the California Caramel machine. I pulled, and the frozen yogurt flowed like honey from a comb. The cup was halfway full when it started to sputter. A groaning buzz, and the light blinked red.

Empty.

FALLING APART

TOM NICHOLSON

When I lost my first finger it was quite a big deal, but by the time the third one detached it was more of a nuisance than anything.

The index said goodbye on the "F" key. It came off at the knuckle and fell behind the office computer. When I found time to fish it out at the end of my shift, the rats had nibbled off most of the skin. I'd typed the word "unfortunately" 36 times that day.

The second finger departed at the printer. I flicked through a stack of papers thrown at me by my line manager, and just like that, it was no more wedding rings. He said it was extremely important that he get 16 copies before brunch time, so it surprised me when he let his assistant sweep away the protuberance with a dustpan and brush before he made an official complaint to H.R. about my performance.

The last finger prevented me from signing the termination notice. I made it through my first name, but the dot over the "i" in my last proved too much and my middle finger split in two, almost providing me with a full complement once more. They told me my typing was too slow but they wished me luck in my future endeavours so that was nice. I heard later that they got quite angry, because they had to hire someone to come and clean the mark I'd left on the coffee table.

A few weeks after I was sitting at home tapping out applications with my remaining digits when a letter arrived from my old company. They told me they were rescinding my severance package because the bloodstains on the table wouldn't come out. I was still under contract at the time of signing so what I did was technically destruction of company property with company property which meant I'd have to pay double damages, so now I needed a new job twice as much.

Good thing I'm a hard worker because less than six months later I was delivering oversized packages that wouldn't fit in postal vans. Losing all those fingers allowed me to be creative with how I got them from my bike, across brick-patterned driveways littered with range rovers and onto people's porches. I had this technique where I would shift them onto my back and sprint as fast as I could before the bones in my knees started to creak. I made sure to include these skills in any cover letter I attached with my resume.

I liked that job while it lasted, but it became untenable when my big toes fell off. No one ever tells you how much they help with balance but you definitely notice when they aren't there anymore. On the plus side, it made it less of an adjustment when my feet fell off pedalling home.

It was hard to find employment after that so I gritted my teeth and took the bus down to the Jobcentre. The woman there was very sweet. She yelled that since I'd technically quit my last job I didn't qualify for any help with paying my bills or feeding my children. When I finished wiping her spit from my eyes I tried to explain that my children quite liked eating and having a roof over their head. Unfortunately, I got a little too emotional and I felt the blood building at the back of my throat. I was trying to say the word "love" when my tongue detached and the force of that against my top teeth made the muscle flick over the desk and land in her lap, which in hindsight might have contributed to security's arrival seconds later.

I pondered what to do back at my house while the children were at school. Thankfully my eyesight was failing so when the sun disappeared outside and we couldn't afford to turn the lights on it didn't matter too much. We sat there in the dark and the quiet. It actually helped us focus and the kids came up with some great ideas for how we could pay rent. They offered to go to work instead, setting up their own delivery service at school and pitching in their lunch money. I didn't have the heart to tell them they were being undercut by outsourcing at my last job.

Just as things were looking their bleakest, the phone rang. I fumbled to pick it up. A local news reporter had heard about my situation and wanted to invite me to speak at the next town council meeting. It felt a little like charity to me so I was hesitant at first. I'm an independent man and I don't need any of that, let me tell you. Given my limitations, she did most of the talking. She wanted me to give a speech about the failings of local government and how more should be done to help people like me. She sounded genuine, so despite my moral concerns I agreed.

The children spent the morning helping me get ready. They stood on each other's shoulders to comb my hair and tie my tie. When I arrived at the town hall the reporter had clearly gone to a lot of effort to accomodate me. I dragged myself up the stone steps and over the gravel pathway, then up through the big oak doors where security patted me down.

I made it onto the stage and delivered my address. An advertiser for the newspaper had paid for a machine to convert my blinks into speech so I could speak to those in attendance about how more money should be spent on helping people rather than on meaningless symbols of caring that had little bearing on the everyday lives of those they were designed to help.

"Good evening," I said, and my words rang out through the hall with a voice far more proper than my own. "Thank you for taking the time to listen to me tonight. I love working. As I've written at the top of hundreds of application letters, even as a child I dreamed of the day I would one day get that first assignment to go and fetch the coffee. If I could, I would work even more, demand more perfection from myself, but we can't always do the things we love. Sometimes our limitations catch up with us, and our own flaws in pushing too hard mean we can't live up to expectations.

"I want you to know that I have no desire to give this speech. I know that, in a modern workplace, it's unrealistic to expect to keep all my appendages. The magnificent increases in productivity we've seen in the last few years mean that the occasional sacrifice is often required just to keep pace, let alone get ahead. But some part of me feels, deep down, that not only me, but all of us truly do deserve some sort of provision for when we lose too many. I'm not asking for another look at the living wage or even a legally mandated minimum amount of care and dignity. There are far more important things for you to consider than that. I only want my kids to eat and to go to school. I'm happy to starve and die in my own filth as long as they get the chance to one day lose their own limbs to fund the loving and caring family that allows them a paycheck. What I'm asking for is not a handout or basic decency or respect, but just a glance, a flickering of emotion behind the eyes that lets me know that maybe one day, far down the line, that flicker might become an idea, and even further away that idea might turn into an action that helps my great, great grandchildren see how much better things might be. If you can give me that, then I can leave here happy. Thank you."

The councillors sat in one row on a long cushioned bench at the other end of the stage. They maintained their ears so I'm sure they heard what I was saying. There was a lot of nodding and nose wrinkling that suggested empathy. I stopped my blinks and the electric voice trailed off. The councillors applauded politely with both hands and started to discuss the absolute necessity of buying new microphones, since it was such an inconvenience struggling to hear one another at each end of their bench.

I think they forgot I was still on the stage because they spoke for a long time. I swivelled my head back and forth trying to focus on each in turn. There were chats about how awful it must be to lose a job and whether they could organise a parade in my honour without cutting into the Christmas party budget. Then the talk turned to the machine provided by the advertiser. They seemed fascinated by it. How it might be adapted for their own needs so they'd no longer have to appear in person to respond to these sorts of speeches.

I'm sure they'd have allocated some funds for my issues eventually. If there'd been time, I'd have blinked for longer. I'd have explained how these failings could happen to anyone, how they compound, once one finger goes it's harder to keep the rest attached as each one takes up the slack, until you're down to nothing, not even the speech from your lungs for functional ears to hear and ignore.

I would have said all that, turning to each of them as they discussed how much might be made from the blinking machine, but just my luck, what with all the swivelling, I felt something snap in my spine and my head sailed across the stage, landing with a bump in the centre aisle of the empty hall.

But enough about me. This is really about how the council got that lovely bust they keep outside the hall. The one they had installed to commemorate the lives lost to poverty and economic bad luck. Everyone agrees it's a potent symbol for the struggle of the working class. It really gives them something to strive towards. The head of one of their own given pride of place in the town.

It cost a fortune to lacquer the flesh and have bits of it reattached when they fell off sweeping it out of the aisle. It still stands now, looking out over an empty car park, one eyebrow raised at the pigeons who don't pay for a ticket, letting everyone who cares know about the hero of labour who once gave a speech about something or other. It's lasted ever so well since they cleaned the droppings off. I suppose that's what happens when you use such lifelike materials. Why waste good marble when you have the real thing right there? I'm lucky. Most people can only dream of being so useful. There's job security too. No one's applying to replace me anytime soon. I get a pat on the head when things go well, and completely ignored when they don't. Who could hope for more purpose in life?

BLUR

DAVID STEVENS

C aleb ducked in from one cubicle to another. Left the phone, the computer, the roving supervisor for a moment of peace on the porcelain. But no more than a moment. They timed this, too.

He cherished the quiet. In a short while, his ears would adjust and pick up the sounds from outside, but for just now, the only noises were his own. There weren't many of those. He thought of the slow movement of continental plates, the gradual attrition of ancient rocks, traces of fine dust.

There were no timers in the toilet. They had shown that to the workplace inspectors. The timers were at their desks —no keyboard tapped, no phone line used for five minutes. Lynette couldn't come in here, it was the Men's, but she had roaming enforcers. *Lackeys*, that was the word he was looking for. If he wasn't back at his desk soon, the outer door would swing open. All of the workplace clatter would flow in. Then it would close, with no sound of footsteps on the tiled floor.

You have been warned.

The urge was there, but nothing was happening. He had to get this over with. Performance anxiety. *Uh...*

There. The welcome void.

Just wait though, in case. It was the coffee. Coffee is poison, why did he drink so much? Because it was there, something to do. They kept it boiling all day, the perfume of percolation permeating the place. He didn't have to drink it. He could cut back. His head ached in anticipation of caffeine withdrawal. Didn't have to go cold turkey, but... intersperse it with tea. Only thing was, they made no allowance for tea. They provided coffee, dripping away all day, not tea, not hot water. No urn, no kettle. He'd have to bring a thermos of it from home. Caleb knew himself. He would make the effort for two days, rally again for a further day later in the week, then give up. *Typical.*

A late surge shocked him back to the present. *Lucky I waited.* No vague meandering of continental drift this time, but a spectacular eruption, quickly over. He panted, light-headed, red faced from the effort. Lucky the external door had not been opened at that moment.

Time to go. *Don't*, but he did. He always did. Curiosity. Checking for symptoms. As he reached to depress the button to flush, he looked.

The toilet was full of soft, fluttering grey moths.

Caleb stared. Gently pulsing, a living fur rug reaching up the side of the bowl.

He would have been less shocked by a litre of blood.

The paper he had dropped was already being drawn down beneath the carpet of them, shifted by their incessant shuffling.

Caleb flushed, then ran. There was no way he was going to be blamed for this.

———

THE SUN HAD long set when he emerged from the call factory. He shuffled into the pharmacy, feeling guilty like he always did. He tried on his "honest, I'm not here to rip anything off" face, but that was the face he used to wear when he was trying to rip stuff off. In the end he just looked distressed and embarrassed, hopping from foot to foot while he waited for all of the old ladies to fill their prescriptions.

"Help ya?" The girl looked as tired as he felt, but she made the effort and gave him a smile. He wasn't so stupid to think it meant she liked him. Not any more, he wasn't. They told them in the call center, "smile when you speak on the phone, you can hear a smile." Caleb reckoned there'd be something wrong with a smile you can hear. Creaking gums, cracking lips, breaking jaws. A smile should be silent. It should suddenly sheen on your face, frictionless. Like on beauty pageant contestants with Vaseline smeared on their teeth. The girl's smile was nice, though. Tired and nice.

"Help ya?"

Don't mumble. "Yeah, I've had crook guts," he said, then paused. *Don't pause, you idiot.* He knew he should have got it all out. *She'll take one look and guess that I'm constipated,* he thought. *We know why she'll think that.* Anger rose. *I don't have to take this. Doesn't matter how hard you try, they keep judging you.*

"There's a bug going round. This'll bind you up." Showing him the bottle, already handy there under the counter. "Don't need a prescription."

It was the opposite of what he expected, but he couldn't leave it alone. "How did you know I needed binding up? Not the other..." *Loosening,* he recalled, but didn't say it.

"That's the bug that's going round. Gives you the runs."

"Oh." He was embarrassed. He had to trust more. So he did. He leaned forward and lowered his voice, like a kid about to ask where the condoms are. She looked wary then for the first time, and jerked back an inch or two. "Do you have anything for… moths?" he asked.

She blinked. Her eyelashes were so fine it was like she didn't have any. "Moths? Like clothes moths?"

"'Spose. Maybe a bit bigger."

She shook her head. "Try the 7-Eleven."

The young bloke working at the corner shop found it for him.

"How's it work?" It was a box. Caleb had expected a pill bottle, or a blister pack.

The man pointed at the side. "There's instructions."

"Oh."

Caleb read them by street lights on the way home, one line per light. The kid was right, you couldn't take it internally. You put it in your pantry (*Larder*, he suddenly thought. That was a word his grandmother used to use. Before she died. *Larder*.), and moths would stick to the side of it. Why stick it in a cupboard? How do the moths know to go there? Do you have to leave the door open for them?

Before he arrived home, he realised that both shop assistants had misunderstood the nature of his problem. Thinking it through, he was glad that they had.

———

CALEB WAS TRYING. He filled his thermos with hot water. He'd forgotten about the business of the day before until he opened the pantry door to grab some tea bags. There were a couple of pissy little moths stuck to the side of the trap, one or two of them still flapping a bit. Tiny things. *Call that a moth? This is a moth…*

About to leave, he went to the bathroom to brush his teeth. By his pillow lay an open copy of *Build Your Vocabulary Every Day*. Across the pillow slip was a thick stain of drool.

Gross, he thought. *Who does that? Can't live like this, man. What if you bring a girl home? Don't worry, not going to happen...*

No, he was wrong. He looked closer at the stain. A long smear of fur. Matted wings and soft, crushed bodies.

———

HER NAME WAS Jan. She spoke to him sometimes in the break room. It was the only place he ever saw her. Caleb didn't press it. He didn't try to make friends at work. He didn't need certain kinds of friends. That was the last thing he needed, more people like him. He briefly recalled the girl from the pharmacy, her smile.

Jan's hands were fluttering, emptying packet after packet of sugar into her coffee. It was piling up on top, taking its time to sink down. She didn't notice.

"You OK?" she asked. *You're not*, he thought, but he just nodded, and sipped at his tea.

"You should go some D. Take the edge off."

Fuck. At work. Shit. "E? Why would I go E? I'm happy in my work, thank you for asking." He said the last sentence a bit louder, to make sure it came out on the microphones. Not that there were any. He'd discussed that in group.

She nodded, drank a mouthful of coffee, grimaced. He knew she said 'D.' She knew he knew. Who would take 'E' at work?

Take the edge off. My arse. That was the opposite of what he remembered. Sharp lines. No fuzzy background, every-thing in focus. Attention to every detail. The whole universe laid out for inspection.

She looked around. He smelled her desperation. Her smile was a hole, stretching to give him a glimpse of the yawning precipice he knew was always there. He walked a tightrope every day, under no illusions.

"Don't you have a program?" he whispered.

She ignored his comment. "It's been two–three–two. That means there's four weeks to the next test." She sniffed. "It's a pattern. You're safe."

So you're a patternmatician. Caleb remained silent. He wasn't part of the conversation. She tipped her head back like a baby bird, and emptied the contents of a sugar sachet into her mouth. Pushing the chair back noisily, she wandered off, distracted, forgetting her coffee.

After lunch, she was gone. Caleb felt bad. There must have been something he could do to help. Later that afternoon, when the doors had all been locked from the outside and they were queued up, girls on the left, boys on the right, peeing in cups, he wondered at her not being there.

––––––

CALEB FLUSHED and flushed and flushed again. The pulpy mass of moths was reduced with each fresh flow of water. He promised God he would never use a work toilet again. Just let him not be noticed this one time. He didn't care if they blocked the drains, didn't care if the sewers clogged up with their flimsy wings. All he cared about was that they didn't blame him for it.

Afterwards, back at his desk, she announced her movements with the clack of her heels, great platforms of cork tied together with rope. It was like she'd had them fixed for tap-dancing, they were that loud. Lynette was slumming it, walking the floor, pissing to mark her territory. He had slipped through a hole in time back to the 70s. Wicker wrapped wine bottles recycled as candle holders. Photographs of his gran and her friends, too short skirts and chunky thighs. That wasn't Lynette though. She was lean and always hungry, and he knew he was in her sights.

Fucki'n leave me alone. Caleb froze as she patrolled, couldn't help it, if she just stayed away he'd get the job done, but where was the fun in that? Hovering, she knew he knew she was there, but he did not want to look up at that horse's head, the toffee drawn skinny face.

"You drinking?"

Was she talking to him? "No. What? Alcohol? No." She asked in front of everyone, like you could just do that.

"What's with the minty fresh routine? You smell like a dentist's."

It just came out. "I figured if the customers..."

"*Clients.*" And she fair dinkum rolled her eyes.

"If the... clients can hear a smile, I wouldn't want them hearing bad oral hygiene."

She stared, but Caleb was without guile. He had never uttered a sarcastic word in his time at the center. His face gave away nothing. In his life he had defied social workers, judges, teachers, parents. She would get nothing from him.

"What kind of loser are you, Caleb?'

He was back on the phone line. *What kind?* The kind you get federal assistance for hiring.

———

IT WAS TRUE. He wasn't a big fan of alcohol. The only thing he was drinking was the mouthwash. More often, instead of spitting after gargling, he was swallowing. Detox. He couldn't drink fly spray, but he figured if mouthwash could kill all the shit in his mouth, it'd kill moths further down.

"I want a big bottle," he said at the pharmacy after the other customers... *clientele...* had gone. He had thought her hair was straight, but he noticed little ringlets forcing their way through.

This time she was the one who lowered her voice,

checking her boss couldn't hear. "You know you can get it cheaper at Woolies."

He was adamant. "I want the strong stuff. Pharmaceutical grade."

She shrugged, didn't meet his eyes. "Don't think you need it."

He blushed, and ran his tongue hard along the back of his teeth, feeling every ridge, every crack. Once outside the store, he realized he could never return. The people he wanted to be friends with, they should never be friends with someone like him.

———

CALEB SAT at his kitchen table, a work manual open face down. He couldn't concentrate on the folder, and made the call instead.

"Meth? Course we did. Is this part of some 12 step program?"

"*Not* meth. I didn't say *meth*." Caleb hung up before the conversation got any more stupid.

———

LYNETTE CHEWED ON A PEN. She was always chewing on something, a pen, a nail, an intern. If he reached out and banged her hand just right, Caleb was pretty sure he could drive the pen up through her soft palate. He didn't think it would penetrate her brain or anything, but it would muck her up a bit. He was breathing anger, hating her so much that his vision was vibrating.

"I don't have to do this."

She shook her head. "No you don't. But…"

"I've done nothing wrong." Cop show words.

"Caleb, we're worried about you." He didn't snort at that, didn't levitate a foot out of the tubular steel chair. "You're demonstrating classic furtive behaviour—swigging mouthwash all the time, you keep leaving the floor... "

"To go to the toilet."

"We have toilets. If you've nothing to hide, just give the blood, and we can get it over with."

He could form the sentences. He had been to night classes. He'd had his teeth fixed. Joined a gym. He could mouth off about intrusion, civil rights, presumption of innocence. Lynette looked at him and her eyes told him otherwise. None of it made a difference. He'd jumped ship from that universe a long time ago and set up residence in a parallel world, where there was no such thing as self-improvement. If he didn't want to sink down to a deeper dimension of shit, he'd shut up and get on with it.

Having nothing to hide, he stuck his arm out, and let them draw the blood, right there in the call center annex.

———

TWO WEEKS LATER, he sat in darkness in a fugue of anger. He would not break. He would not submit. He was no stereotype. That didn't mean he wasn't so fucking angry he couldn't tear down the whole building. That he wouldn't head out soon and buy a packet of cigarettes. He was tugging his hair up out of his head. *All that effort...*

Sometime in the night, she was there. He didn't remember opening the door. He was suddenly sick like the old days, in his guts and in his head, and somewhere deep inside. Bright light was behind her, a grey descending from the mother ship, ready with the anal probe. Then he saw it was Jan.

She didn't look like a junky today. Her hair was brushed

back off her face, held in a bun. Her skin was clean, her clothes ironed. She was plonked on a kitchen chair, earnest.

"Listen to me. My sister's running some kind of angle here. She's not fired you for no reason. You've got the rights to all the blood results. In the morning, you call this number and ask them to send your medical file."

Lynette hadn't been at the meeting when they dismissed him. It wasn't like her to miss a chance to lord it over some sucker getting the sack. Something was going on. Just a skinny nervy bloke, stumbling over his name.

"It's a federal program. It might be a crap job, but health care is mandatory."

After she left, all he thought was: *Sister?*

———

HOPE WAS a wicked bugger that he tried to keep at bay. It had never been a friend to him, and he was in danger of being overwhelmed by it now.

Caleb had never been upstairs at the call center before. There was a view. They probably had a view downstairs as well, except the blinds were always drawn. The difference between working in a mine and managing a mine, he supposed.

When he turned around in his seat he could see the pharmacy and the 7-Eleven. Couldn't see inside the pharmacy window, though he tried.

Lynette was here this time, but he tried not to look at her. The skinny guy who fired him was there too, but not at the table. He sat at the back, nursing a briefcase, rocking like he wanted to run. The coffee they were brewing smelled heaps better than downstairs.

The old fellow was new. He looked scary, but he spoke nice. Called him "Mister." Offered coffee. "No? Tea if you'd prefer." Caleb didn't want to appear too demanding, so he said no to both. He'd hate to have to make a dash for the toilet.

"We want you to know," the old man began, "that our decision to let you go was not an easy one. You are—were —a valued employee, but there are market forces at work, you understand. Our parting of the ways, let me assure you, just in case a nasty thought had flittered through your mind for a moment—just to relieve you of any concerns—had nothing to do with your blood testing, or the results of that." The man paused and Caleb thought he was going to turn and stare at Lynette, but he just looked straight up in the air, like doing some weird prayer. "On reflection, we have all decided that that is not a course we would take again. I will say how appreciative we are of your role in that affair, the spirit of cooperation you showed. It goes without saying—though I am saying it, of course—how sad we are at the results of that test. Now, I want you to hear this Caleb—you were in our employ at the relevant time so regardless of our... departure from one another, your health insurance will be honoured, and we can put this behind us."

Caleb was eyeing-off the fancy biscuits. He wished he had taken the coffee. He didn't want it, but he thought it would look funny if he just took a biscuit without having a coffee. Might have looked rude after the speech.

"So, I can come back to work then?"

The old silver head did turn right round to Lynette this time, and he looked at her as he spoke to Caleb. Lynette looked away, but not embarrassed or anything, just pissed off. "Have you discussed your test results with a doctor?"

"They haven't arrived yet. An hour after I rang up about them, I got a call about this meeting."

"I see. Caleb, you can be assured there will be some

changes around here. Things will be run differently from today onwards. There is one thing though."

"Yeah?"

The man slid a pen and a piece of paper across the table. "It would be a big help to me if you would sign this, please. It's just about how we've had this chat and cleared up any misunderstanding."

Caleb wanted to please. He wanted to help. He wanted to come back. He took the pen. Somewhere, in another universe, there might have been a union rep next to him, shaking his head, *no*. Hell, a zillion galaxies away, there might have been a version of him with a fancy lawyer. But not here.

He probably would have signed. He bent to do it, but could not stop. As he leaned, he kept going, the full ten thousand miles to the floor. He tasted blood. The old man's cultured voice followed him all the way.

"Fuck Lynette, look what you've done. We'll all be in the shit now."

Lying down there, he heard the doors closing inside his head, one after another, dozens and dozens, in world after world. All his plans, all his efforts, all gone now.

———

"I'm problematic," Jan admitted. "Complex. There is more going on here than you can know."

Caleb nodded. He wanted to be outside, feeling the breeze, finishing his smoke. He didn't recall her asking whether she could wheel him back into the building. He didn't even recall coming back inside.

"I'm very sorry," she said, her hands clasped between her knees. She looked away. "This is the best of all possible worlds. I've tried, but there's no good ending that doesn't somehow require an outcome like this for you."

"Tried everything?" he asked, puzzled.

"Yes," she nodded. "Well, not literally. Not every possible world. I can't go out much further with this. We're not exactly at the center of things here. Further out, it gets too anomalous. Fortean. And frankly, after all this time, we really do have to get a move on. Let's be realistic."

As she spoke, a fluttering in his ear increased, as though something was trapped deep. He did not react; he didn't want her to know. Caleb was tired. Mind drifting, he imagined the same conversation being played out a million million times, at first with the slightest variation, until a billion Chinese whispers away, he was not even human— there was a kettle speaking with a fish.

He was going to need morphine soon. Government supplied, state administered. At one stage he had smiled at the irony. Now, he didn't feel like smiling very much at all any more. He did know that it was unsafe to let Jan think he was not paying her the fullest attention.

"You're caught between forces you cannot understand."

"It's just… just a call center."

"Not if my sister is involved, it isn't."

"Geez, just a job." He rose out of his seat a little at the end, shifting his weight in the chair. He was distracted by movement within, nerve endings reacting to the actions of the malformed cells. And she was the one who was pissed off. She didn't know what Lynette was up to, but she still wanted to fuck with her. There was fire in her eyes; he sensed the anger that could pour out. Then she softened, finally picking up on the cue of his pain.

"The war with my sister has been going on for a very long time. Forever." She leaned forward. "I'm sorry, but in all wars, there is collateral damage. It doesn't have to end like this." She sighed, the model of compassion. "I can stay a while. A little while. Make it pleasant." She looked up and her hair had lightened, her face now plump with a tired smile, and an approximation of the pharmacist's assistant was in the room with him. He felt sick, not just at the pain, but gritted his teeth not to show it. She touched his knee, hinting at a promise he prayed she'd never keep. "Or I can make it like you never existed. The pain, the worry all gone." She was indifferent to whether he chose ersatz pleasure or oblivion, except that oblivion probably interfered with her plans less.

"Thanks," he said, his face the best simulacrum of gratitude he could manage in the circumstances. He wondered if he had even a fraction of the attention of the thing in front of him, with all her planning and conspiring. How many conversations was it having right this moment? How small a part of it was in the room with him? "I'm right. I'll... I'll see it through to the end. On my own. Thanks. I'd rather."

He felt the weight of her gaze, her observation pressing down on him, working out whether she... it... should accept his decision. He was reduced to a butterfly on a slide. Then a moment later she was gone, and the oppression lifted.

She would not be back. He was free.

Caleb sighed. He was too tired to wheel himself back outside, and there was no smoking allowed in the rooms. Through a large window, he could see the light towers bearing down on a night match at the Sydney Cricket Ground. Closer, through the bars he watched the dancing haze of bogong moths as, their migration interrupted, they dashed and dashed themselves against the security lights of the hospital.

Oh well, he thought, *why not?*

He shuffled out of the chair to the wall of his room. It was a warm night, but he kept the beanie on, now that his hair was all gone. What now?

His skin fluttered as his edges blurred. Tiny moths emerged from his pores, wings blurred with movement.

They broke into smaller and smaller units, moths all the way down. Shuddering, he managed another step forward, and was only mildly surprised to find himself penetrating the wall. The tiny moths passed between the molecules of the building, through paint and plaster and more slowly through the fired clay of red brick. They made their way through the cement render all together, the shape of a shivering Caleb still holding, ancient instincts driving, their navigational system still working.

After all that, the sky is nothing to them. His children bear him away. He rises, the chemotherapy emptied husk of him, his perimeter no longer strictly defined. *Why me?* he thinks. This grace is unearned, but the constant flutter of his children reassures him. He is no longer aware of darkness. The night sky is full of lights calling him on, blinking like an ancient switchboard of signals waiting to be connected by a busy operator, their summons more urgent than the ringing of any call center telephone.

Grace unearned, but not undeserved. A wretch like him. Stars urge him beyond the bounds of any open plan cubicle, to join the migration.

So off he goes.

THE PRICE OF MOTHERHOOD
TIFFANY MICHELLE BROWN

For the bargain price of $79,999.95, which she would pay in monthly installments of $99.95 for the next 66 years (not including interest), Leslie Dawson became a mother.

The day the courier arrived, Leslie wore her most responsible-looking outfit, which she'd bought at Goodwill especially for the occasion: a blue button-up, khaki pants, and a string of fake pearls. The cotton material was stiff and scratchy, but Leslie resisted the urge to change into her regular uniform of jeans and a T-shirt. She knew first impressions were important. She needed to resemble the epitome of domesticity today, even if only for a paid delivery person.

When she heard footsteps ascending the stairwell in her apartment complex, Leslie leaped from the couch and opened her door before the representative from Lyfelike had the opportunity to knock.

On the threshold, Leslie's smile dropped, and her heart clenched. She hadn't expected her baby to arrive in a silver, egg-shaped case that reflected the cheap fluorescents in the hallway. When she'd pictured this day in her mind, she'd imagined the courier showing up with the baby strapped to their chest via a Baby Bjorn or pushed in a stroller. There had *never* been an egg.

"Leslie Dawson, it's a pleasure. My name is Matthew, and I'm from Lyfelike. Are you ready to meet your daughter?" The man shoved the egg toward her, zooming right past pleasantries and straight to business. The abruptness left Leslie rattled, and she simply stared until the silence grew awkward.

She cleared her throat and gave him a warm smile. "Absolutely. Won't you come in?" She'd made Crystal Light lemonade and microwaved some cookies she'd found on sale at the grocery store.

"I'm afraid I can't," Matthew said, his voice warm and booming. "It's against company protocol. But I do have a few instructions to share and of course, I'll stay long enough to ensure all is in order."

Leslie hazarded a glance down the hallway. Matthew was quite loud, and she was afraid one of her neighbors would emerge to *shoosh* them. And what would they see? Why, they'd see this man handing her a huge silver egg while she stood there dumbly in her imposter pearls. Leslie's cheeks flushed as she took the egg from Matthew.

"Is it okay for me to set this down?" she asked. "It's a bit heavy." It wasn't, but she longed to tuck the egg inside the apartment. Safe from prying eyes.

"Of course. While you do, a few instructions. Inside the package, there's an instruction manual. It's *very* important that you read the manual, front to back, and dial in all of your preferred settings via your smartphone before you initiate your daughter's heartbeat."

Leslie blinked. Initiate her heartbeat? What the hell did that mean?

Her face must have betrayed her confusion, because Matthew gave her a good-natured chuckle. "It's not a difficult process, I assure you. It'll make sense once you've read the manual. Again, make sure you dial *everything* in beforehand as certain settings can only be adjusted by our team after she's alive. We can, of course, help you troubleshoot any issues you encounter, but in extreme cases, we'd have to reset her completely, and that would mean a reversion back to factory settings." Matthew filled his lungs with fresh air. "It's a pain."

Clinical. Technical. Purchased.

The words beat around inside Leslie's skull like an unwelcome ping pong ball. This was *not* the experience she'd hoped for—or what had been promised on that late-night infomercial she'd seen last year. Lyfelike billed itself as a company that created artificial intelligence entities that were more human than robot. Less computer, more life.

So where was the warmth? Where was the sweep of emotion she'd expected to feel? Matthew's instructions were stripping her resolve. Did she really want this?

She decided she would call Lyfelike later to ask about their return policy. For now, she'd pay attention and be agreeable—don't shoot the messenger and all. While Matthew's bedside manner could use some work, Leslie figured he was following a script, and she couldn't fault him for doing his job.

"Okay, got it." Leslie nodded, hoping she looked attentive and capable.

"That all being said, there are a few settings that may shift naturally as part of your daughter's programming. This will be in response to stimulus, learning, development, that sort of thing. After all, your daughter is meant to be very Lyfelike." He accentuated the final word, and Leslie resisted the urge to roll her eyes. "We want you to enjoy the full spectrum of the parenting experience, so be sure you give her the same level of care you would a human baby. You can monitor all of her settings in the Lyfelike app, and if they shift, refer back to the manual to see what she needs. If you have questions, call our customer service team."

"Sounds good."

"Would you like to ensure your daughter's appearance meets your expectations?"

Dear God, did he just ask her that? And did he expect her to check off a list or something? Blue eyes, great! Freckle on her temple. Yep, just where I requested it.

This was all way too weird.

Matthew smiled pleasantly, and beneath his congeniality, Leslie detected determination. He wouldn't leave until she'd opened the egg and proclaimed all was as it should be. Shit.

Leslie squatted next to the door and cracked open the silver case. The baby was nestled in purple silk and swaddled in soft cotton. Dark curls swooped across her forehead, the perfect frame for her round, pudgy face. Even in the shabby light of the apartment, her skin looked soft as rose petals.

Leslie felt tears building behind her eyes. A smile overtook her lips.

This is what she'd been waiting for. *This* is what she'd had in mind when she'd placed the order with Lyfelike twelve months prior. All of her reservations melted away as she gazed at the infant.

She swatted at her eyes and peered up at Matthew. "She's perfect."

THE STARTUP MANUAL was one hundred and seven pages long, the type was small, and the wording was overly technical. Leslie read ten pages before a sharp pain flashed through her forehead and she realized she was squinting. To make matters worse, she hadn't retained a single word. She'd have to start again.

Leslie made herself a cup of tea, grabbed a sleeve of mini donuts, and flipped back to the beginning of the manual. At page twenty, Leslie pushed back from the table and sighed. She circled her shoulders, trying to release tension from her body. She'd been more successful this time around, but her progress was slow. She doubted she'd be able to read the manual in a single sitting. At this rate, it would take days.

She looked at Annalea, her new daughter, resting on a kitchen chair nearby. She was still swaddled, still "sleeping"— in Leslie's mind, this sounded much better than "not yet powered up." Urgency skittered through her fingers.

She picked up her phone and powered up Instagram. As if the universe knew exactly what she was looking for, Ryan's latest post appeared at the top of her timeline, a family portrait that made her throat close. Ryan had his arm around his new wife, Pauline, a redhead with freckles who somehow managed to look effortlessly beautiful all the time. She held their one-year-old boy, Cash, in her long arms. The boy looked nothing like his mother and everything like his father. Leslie could see Ryan in the slope of the boy's nose, the dark shock of hair that crowned his head, his ice-blue eyes.

As Leslie stared at the picture, something cracked deep within her.

She crammed the last donut in her mouth, licked powdered sugar from her fingers, and closed Instagram. She launched the Lyfelike app and searched through its interface. There had to be a quick-start guide somewhere, right?

Thirty minutes later, Leslie had scoured the website to no avail. In their FAQs section, there was a question about quick-starts, but all it said was to read the manual in full before initiating the heartbeat.

This is some bullshit, Leslie thought, her frustration building. How did anyone have the patience to go through all of this? She'd already waited longer for her daughter to arrive than if she'd actually been pregnant. She needed to be a mother *now*.

On the home screen, Leslie tapped the "Initiate Setup" button. A warning popped up. Had she read the manual in full? It was an imperative step in the process, and blah, blah, blah...Leslie closed the window. The app informed her that the configuration would take fifteen minutes to complete.

Fifteen minutes, Leslie thought. *In fifteen minutes, I'll meet my daughter.*

Some of the settings were easy to choose. Leslie only wanted to change diapers five times a day and she could schedule their frequency down to the minute. She also wanted her daughter to sleep a full eight hours each night. The choices for temperament, goals, and bonding style were more esoteric, but Leslie chose with her gut.

She could read up on all of these choices later. Besides, Lyfelike had a customer service team. If there were any major errors, she would ask them to fix it. She was certainly paying them enough—and with money she didn't truly have —so she expected fantastic service.

Temperament? Good-natured, because who doesn't love a good-natured baby?

Life goal? Peace, which was vague, but sounded more than okay.

Bonding style? Secure, of course.

Fourteen minutes later, Leslie's thumb hovered over "Initiate Heartbeat." A single tear slid down her cheek as she tapped the screen and waited.

LESLIE'S PHONE CHIRPED, announcing a new notification. She balanced Annalea in the crook of her left arm and held her phone close to her face. She'd surpassed two hundred likes on Instagram, and the sudden sweep of validation made her blood hum.

Leslie had nearly forgotten how incredible it felt to be recognized.

Following her Lyfelike purchase twelve months prior, Leslie had abstained from posting to social media with any kind of regularity. She'd still post from time to time, but only strategically angled headshots or photos of knick-knacks in her cramped apartment. Never a full body shot. Never anything telling. She wanted Annalea to be a complete and utter surprise.

She also didn't plan to tell anyone her daughter was from Lyfelike. Rather, she'd tell everyone she'd successfully conceived thanks to a sperm donor.

She'd done the work, and now it was time to shine.

She'd taken nearly forty photos, trying to snap the perfect selfie and then using her smartphone's timer to get a better angle and wider shot. Throughout the photoshoot, Annalea stretched in her swaddling. She smacked her lips as she slept. Her little chest rose and fell. It was easy to believe she was made of blood and bone rather than metal and wiring.

Seconds after the upload, her phone erupted with congratulations and compliments. And now, a comment from Ryan: "She's beautiful, Les. We couldn't be happier for you. Motherhood looks good on you."

For the past two years, whenever she thought of Ryan, Leslie had heard him in her head telling her that it was okay, they weren't meant to have children. He still loved her.

Then, that IVF was far too expensive; even if they were successful, would they be able to financially care for their child amid all the medical bills?

Finally, he didn't love her anymore. Her obsession with motherhood had dulled her, turned her into someone else, someone he didn't know. He'd found Pauline. He was going to marry her. They were expecting a son.

But now, Leslie could replace all of those whispers of the past with newfound validation: *Motherhood looks good on you.*

Leslie poured herself a glass of boxed wine, snuggled into the couch with Annalea on her chest, and closed her eyes. It was the first moment of peace she'd experienced in two years.

———

LESLIE SCROLLED through the Lyfelike app as Annalea wailed in her arms. For something so small, she certainly had volume—volume Leslie hoped she could decrease or even mute. That had to be possible with AI, right?

Leslie couldn't find volume settings, but she did discover a list of sound selections. She flipped through them as the baby continued to cry, the pitch, timbre, and octave switching as she touched her screen. Every choice grated her nerves.

How had it come to this? How, when everything had started so well?

The first two months had been bliss. Leslie's neighbors assumed she'd adopted a baby and lavished her with gifts for the newborn—patterned onesies, jar after jar of baby food, a breast pump (a well-meaning gift, but completely superfluous), home-cooked meals, everything she could possibly need as a new mother. Of course, Leslie let them believe what they wanted to and happily accepted each gift.

Thanks to her neighbors, she delighted in feeding Annalea pureed peas and sweet potatoes during their first month as mother and daughter, though nourishment was entirely optional for Lyfelike infants. She dressed Annalea in darling outfits festooned with roses and ruffles and bows. She even enjoyed tending to Annalea's diaper changes since she knew exactly when her daughter would need a fresh one *and* whether she'd be going number one or number two. Before bed each night, Leslie consulted the Lyfelike app to ensure her daughter was "well," which of course meant functioning properly.

However, as the surprise and novelty of Annalea's arrival decreased, Leslie found it difficult to stick to the routine she'd initially established. When the baby food gifted to her by her neighbors ran out, she didn't make an effort to purchase more. Since it wasn't a requirement, Leslie figured Annalea could do without it.

She'd lost track of diaper-changing times, too. Yes, they happened every day with clockwork accuracy, but they were less of an *event* now. During the first few months, Leslie had anticipated Annalea's changing times, often placing the baby on her changing table and arming herself with a wipe before her daughter did her business. Now, she relied on the baby crying to tell her she needed a change.

And despite the sleep setting Leslie had selected before initiating Annalea's heartbeat, the baby had begun waking in the middle of the night. When she woke, she cried and cried and cried.

Leslie finally consulted her Lyfelike app, which she'd also been neglecting as of late, and discovered that Annalea's settings had changed dramatically. Her Good-Natured temperament now read as Distressed. Her life goal was Survival. Her bonding style was Anxious-Preoccupied, whatever that meant.

And now, she wouldn't stop crying. Leslie changed Annalea's diaper, tried to sing her a lullaby, spooned a bit of canned soup into her mouth, but nothing worked. Leslie didn't know what the hell the baby needed, and the constant bawling was driving her mad.

She scrolled to the bottom of the Lyfelike app, memorized the customer service number, and punched it into her phone. As the phone rang, Annalea's blubbering grew more and more desperate, as if she somehow sensed in her little robot brain that her mother was about to complain about her.

Annalea's screams were so piercing, Leslie didn't hear the customer service rep when they came on the line. Or when they asked how they could help. She didn't hear a thing until the rep started spouting off a scripted goodbye: "Thank you for calling Lyfelike, where we bring home to you." And then the line went dead.

"Dammit," Leslie shouted and chucked her phone on the couch. She marched to the bathroom, Annalea in her arms. She set the baby on the tile floor, her jaw clenched in frustration, her breath coming hard through her nose.

Annalea's face was red and splotchy. A pang of guilt shot through Leslie like lightning.

Damn the people at Lyfelike for doing this. For making Annalea so convincing. For making Leslie feel like a godawful mother.

Leslie caught her reflection in the dark glass above the sink. She looked like hell. There were bags under her eyes, her hair looked like a motel for rodents, and her lips were turned down in an exhausted grimace.

"I just need a minute," she said, her voice trembling.

She left the bathroom and closed the door behind her.

———

"It sounds like she'll need a manual override," the Lyfelike rep said over the phone. "I'm looking at her settings right now. Any idea how this happened?"

"None," Leslie said. "I've taken exceptional care of her." The lie was oily on her tongue, but she wasn't about to be lambasted by a customer service rep for her parenting skills.

"Okay, let's get someone out to you as soon as possible."

"That sounds wonderful," Leslie said.

"Looks like the earliest appointment we have available is Wednesday between 9 AM and 1 PM."

Leslie frowned. Why did it feel like she was scheduling an appointment to have a contractor over to fix a leaky faucet? And two more days of having to deal with a malfunctioning robot baby? Unacceptable.

"You don't have anything sooner?" Leslie tried hard to keep the edge out of her voice, but it was there, sharp and dark.

"You could contact our ServicePro team," the rep said. "They would likely be able to send someone out to you today."

Relief flooded through Leslie, but before she could say yes, this was exactly what she wanted, the Lyfelike rep continued.

"However, access to our ServicePro team is only available for an additional fee."

Leslie's chest tightened. *You've got to be kidding me.* "And that fee is...?"

"$99.95 per call, ma'am."

"Are you serious?" Pain sliced through Leslie's temple, the onset of a stress migraine. "One hundred dollars for a single call? Even though I'm already paying you that much monthly?"

"It's a separate service, ma'am."

"How is this ethical? You're dealing with people's *lives*

here! And stop calling me ma'am. It's condescending." Leslie's voice was ragged, her chest burned, and her whole body shook. "I bought something that was *really* expensive and that I shouldn't have purchased in the first place. It's not working out, and it shouldn't be this goddamn hard!"

Silence floated through the line as Leslie reined in her breathing.

"I'm sorry, Leslie. Can I call you that?"

"Sure."

"I'll submit this with a note that if any cancellations come through, your request receives priority. Unless, of course, you'd like me to connect you with ServicePro?"

"Does it sound like I want the help from ServicePro?"

"Understood, Leslie. Is there anything else I can do for you?"

"No."

"Thank you for calling Lyfelike, where we bring home to you."

———

MIRACULOUSLY, after Leslie hung up with Lyfelike, her apartment was blissfully quiet. She assumed that Annalea, much like real, human infants, had tired herself out. She would let her sleep as long as she needed.

In the interim, she'd try to do some research. Leslie flipped through the pages of Annalea's instruction manual until she found the section with setting descriptions.

A Distressed temperament was easy enough to understand. Annalea wasn't getting the level of care she needed, so she was fussy and irritable. It was meant to be a signal for the owner to increase their level of care and attention.

The Survival life goal meant that Annalea was doing

whatever was necessary to thrive. Her independence and personal initiative were higher than they should be.

The Anxious-Preoccupied bonding style was character-ized by four heavy phrases: emotional hunger, fantasy bond, lack of nurturing, and turbulence.

The manual slipped from Leslie's fingers and tumbled to the dirty carpet as realization struck her. She'd failed, hadn't she? Annalea's settings had shifted because she'd been doing a shitty job, not because the AI technology was malfunction-ing. Leslie had wanted this for so long, and now... she couldn't cut it.

The air suddenly felt suffocating in the apartment. Leslie ran to the nearest window, threw it open, and took five deep breaths.

Could she turn this around? Surely she could learn from this failure and strive to be better, right? She had to. She had to succeed at this.

She screwed her eyes shut and called forward her memo-ries. The painful ones, the joyful ones, everything that had brought her to this moment. Making love to Ryan and feeling like this was it, the time they'd conceive naturally, only to see those two dreaded lines on a pregnancy test the following month. The bottles of wine she'd drowned in when he'd left her. That little stir of hope in her womb when she'd seen the Lyfelike infomercial. The way she'd finally felt complete when she first held Annalea in her arms.

She could do this. She could be a good mother. She simply had to remember and rebuild.

Leslie's phone dinged. She pulled the device from her pocket, opened Instagram, and squinted at the new photo posted on Ryan's account. The image was confusing at first. She was staring at a cropped body shot of a woman wearing jeans, her red T-shirt pulled up to expose her midriff. There was nothing exceptional or strange or disturbing or magical about the belly on display.

But when she read the caption, adrenaline threatened to scald Leslie's insides.

"Coming soon! We're hoping for a girl this time. #ProudPapa"

Pauline was pregnant again. The belly was hers, and beneath her creamy, freckled skin, a baby was growing inside her.

The newfound motivation Leslie had cultivated just moments ago dimmed, and her sense of failure flared anew.

Her body had betrayed her. Finances kept her from creating a family with the man she'd once loved. And now, Leslie had *bought* a child.

And for what?

She trudged to her kitchen, rifled through her cupboards, and pulled out the bottle of cheap gin she kept in case of emergencies. Leslie sunk into the couch cushions, staring at Pauline's belly and the joyous comments accumulating under the post. She tipped back the bottle until everything blurred.

———

LESLIE AWOKE to the sound of someone screaming, a bright, shrill cry that jarred her senses. She tried to open her eyes, but the light streaming into her apartment was too harsh. Her pulse beat against her skull, and an unsettling pressure weighed heavily on her chest.

Was she having a panic attack? No, there was something on top of her. Something warm and moving.

Annalea!

Leslie forced her eyes open. Annalea's mouth was wide and angry as she bellowed, her breath hot on Leslie's face. A deluge of tears streamed down the baby's cheeks as she squirmed and kicked, tried to burrow deeper into the warmth of her mother.

But it was the state of her hands that sucked all the breath from Leslie's chest. Annalea's tiny palms were smeared with a red substance that resembled blood. A good deal of her fake skin had peeled back, revealing an intricate maze of metal and wiring. The mechanical digits flexed as they searched for Leslie's skin. When they found an acceptable place, the fingers dug in, and Leslie felt a flash of bright, hot pain shuttle through her.

Even as the pain grew, Leslie gazed upon Annalea with wonder. Beneath the horror of this situation, another sensation welled up inside her, something strong and sure that she couldn't quite pinpoint.

"Sweet baby," she whispered. "My girl, my girl, my girl—"

Leslie pulled Annalea from her chest and sat up. Rivers of blood poured down her arms and slicked the skin beneath her T-shirt, but Leslie paid her injuries no mind. She was focused on Annalea. She bounced her baby and cooed, trying to get her daughter's cries under control. She wiped blood from Annalea's face, unsure if it was the synthetic stuff Lyfelike had injected into Annalea's stainless steel veins or her own. She examined Annalea's hands gently.

Her poor baby. Her poor, sweet baby.

And Annalea *was* hers, she reminded herself. This beautiful infant belonged to her, regardless of how she'd come by her. Screw all the pregnant bellies and people with more money and, therefore, access to biological science and everyone who knew how to do this parenthood thing right from the get-go. They had nothing to do with her relationship with Annalea. Absolutely nothing.

"It's okay, sweetheart," Leslie said, pulling Annalea closer still. "You found me. You found me, and I'm never letting you go."

Leslie swiped tears from her cheeks. She looked to the bathroom door, already knowing what she would find.

There was a hole in the door, the product of something scrabbling at the wood for hours on end. Smudges of red patterned the floor of Leslie's apartment, forming a trail from the bathroom door to the couch. Motherly pride capsized her heart.

She came for me, Leslie thought. *She needs me. She needs her mother. And I need her.*

As if in response, Annalea reached up and fisted the skin on Leslie's cheek. The infant's fingers disappeared beneath flesh. And in that moment, Leslie didn't feel pain. She felt something so much sweeter: connection.

It was a perfect moment, a moment that needed to be captured.

Wincing, Leslie lifted her phone and smiled.

ALABASTER CITIES
JOANNA MICHAL HOYT

W hat I'm about to tell you isn't a pipe dream or a senile hallucination, understand? I am not and never have been a drinking or a drugging man. I'm only sixty-eight, and my faculties are intact. Ed Sievwright wasn't that much older than I am, and he was sane and sober too, and had his share of common sense. He was a good farmer, too. My kind of good farmer, I mean: small and smart. He and Mary Agnes worked their own land with their own hands and knew what they were about. The soil was getting deeper, not shallower, on their fields, and they managed pretty much to keep out of debt until Mary Agnes got so sick. The doctors couldn't do that much for her, but Ed put all the money he had into trying to get her put right, and then he borrowed the money he didn't have against the farm he did have. And then the crash came. I guess the bank had gambled away what they had, and they foreclosed on Ed's place and too many others to get it back. Did nicely for themselves too, I guess, with that big new mall going in where Ed's fields used to be.

I thought Ed would move away then, go join one of his

kids in the cities. But it seems he couldn't go far from what had been his place, no matter how he hated what they did to it. He got him a job at the hardware store, and another job delivering papers, and a third job that nobody paid him for but that he showed up for, regular as clockwork: walking by his old place and mourning every single thing ruined there. Not just the house and the barn, but the stream and the pastureland, and the hayfield, and the scrubby meadow that he'd let run wild for the woodcocks and the butterflies. He watched while every last bit of it got bulldozed and paved over, and then he said there wasn't a thing left to wreck. He stayed away until the mall building was up and open. Then he started going back again. He never went inside, but he stood in the parking lot sometimes and watched the people going in and out. When I asked him why, he said, "I was wrong. There's still something left to wreck, and they're wrecking it. Just look at those people's faces!" Well, I thought he was just holding a grudge about the farm.

I still thought that when he told me he'd spotted something uncanny about the new mall, and about the bank building too. (Oh yes, he kept on going to the same bank—what else was he going to do? It was the only one in town, and once he'd lost the land he needed money for everything.)

First he said those buildings were too clean. I didn't pay that much mind. It used to be that he kept his barn clean and Mary Agnes kept their house clean, and he didn't learn her side of the work. After she passed, the house was getting to be a sight even before he lost it. As for the apartment, even Mary Agnes might not have been able to keep that place really clean. So I thought it was just the contrast getting to him. But he harped on the new buildings being "unnatural clean" till I started noticing how shiny-white the outside walls were all the time, and how I never saw anyone washing them.

Then he said the bank was growing.

"Hiring more people?" I said. "Maybe they'll get a decent one in by mistake."

"Not adding people," Ed said. "And the people weren't the problem anyway. Beulah's a good neighbor on her own account, and Tim too; they brought casseroles when Mary Agnes was sick, and they helped me move my stuff out when I... when... Anyway. Even Randy isn't bad if you get him away from work. It's the place that's wrong, I tell you. The building. It's growing."

I told him I hadn't seen anyone making additions.

"Nobody's making additions," Ed said. "It's just growing on its own."

I'm sorry to say I laughed.

Just a month ago, in early September, Ed came over with a paper and showed me the measurements he'd taken from the front steps to the sidewalk. One measurement a month, starting in May. Every month that distance shrank by a couple of inches. Now, Ed was better than a hugger-mugger carpenter; he knew how to measure right.

"How do you know the sidewalk's not growing?" I asked, just being a smart aleck. So Ed showed me the measurements from the bank's back door to the chain-link fence by the churchyard. Those were shrinking too, at about the same rate. That got me rattled, and I started measuring too. The measurement I got out front was half an inch shy of the last one he'd recorded. Just when I was noting it down, Randy Fisk—that's the branch manager for the bank—came out, gave me the hairy eyeball, and asked what I was doing.

"Writing," I said, which I was by then.

"Why are you writing here?" he asked.

"It's my First Amendment right to write wherever I want to," I said, and he just shrugged and went in. But it struck me his shirt was just a little too bright and too clean—the wrong kind of white, if you follow me—and his face almost the same color. That gave me a turn. But the next time I saw him at church he looked all right, no paler than you'd expect a man to be who's shut in all day, and I thought I'd been imagining things. He was friendly enough too, then. I thought of what Ed had told me: the people weren't the problem. If there really was anything wrong besides an old man's morbid imagination, like as not it was something the bank had done to Randy, not something he had done to it.

I didn't have much time to brood over that, because Jake —that's my youngest brother—started calling me up or stopping by in the evenings and complaining about how much time his kids were spending at that new mall. Wasn't natural, he said. Judy'd given up practicing her violin, and she used to love that, and Jimmy'd stopped playing soccer, and neither one of them was doing homework or chores so's you'd notice.

Well, since Jimmy was seventeen and Judy fourteen, I figured they were just being naturally miserable and slouching off the way they seem to feel obliged to do just about the time they turn old enough to be useful. But Ed kept on at me about it until I stopped at the mall to have a look at what they were doing.

Judy was with a gaggle of girls looking at horrible clothes with next to no cloth in them that cost as much as if they were four times the size and cloth of gold to boot. Jimmy was lined up with a bunch of boys outside the video game booth, standing around waiting his turn (judging by the posters on the outside) to shoot imaginary bullets at imaginary terrorists to save imaginary blondes that were wearing clothes just like those ones Judy'd been gawping at. Both of them said "Hi, Uncle Lendel," when I came up to them, but then they turned right away again like they didn't care to know me. They looked awful pale. Too much time inside, I thought.

And then I thought again about that kind of white shine on the walls of the mall and the bank, and then I thought about Randy Fisk's face. I told myself I was getting to be a foolish old man. I didn't mention my notions to Jake; he was already worried enough.

But Ed, he called me again the next week—that's the week before last—saying he'd bought a video camera and read about how they do that time-lapse photography thing, like in movies when the clouds go flying over and you know they've just skipped a bunch of dull parts and the next big thing's about to happen. He aimed to show how the bank was growing.

He came over the next day, just crestfallen. Randy Fisk had told him he didn't have permission to take video footage at the bank. Randy had called the police when Ed didn't want to leave. Ed said he'd go back at night when Randy wasn't there to see, and he'd set up a camera someplace it wouldn't show—he had a tree in mind.

That was the last time I saw Ed. The next day there was a new flowerbed in front of the bank with a white stone statue in the middle of it. I called Ed to ask what he thought of it. He didn't answer. I went to his house. He wasn't there. I called and I went over every day for a week, and I called his kids, and I called everyone he might have gone to visit. Nobody knew where he was. I called the police. They said he might just have decided to go on a trip. I started getting the nastiest notion that somebody'd killed Ed and buried him under that statue.

I was studying on that when I noticed something funny about the statue. The plaque said it was James Tilney, that so-called war hero that Marge Tilney—the mayor's cousin—brags on for her ancestor and brings up whenever anyone tries to criticize any war, but the statue wasn't standing at attention, not quite. Oh, he was straight-backed like Ed always was and like you might expect any soldier to be, but his right foot was rolled in just the same as Ed's, and that's not what you'd look for in a soldier, at least not in a statue of one. And that's not all. That statue's right index finger was exactly the same length as his right middle finger, and that's not a common thing. Marge Tilney's fingers are nothing like that, but Ed Sievwright's were. The statue even had skinny upper arms and fat forearms like Ed had. Only his face wasn't like Ed's face at all, just a blank staring thing in that shining white stone.

I went on into the bank, all set to keep after the bank folks with questions about where that statue had come from. I stepped in, and the door closed behind me, and I got a nasty turn. Tim and Beulah looked at me from behind the counter, and Randy from his desk over in the corner, and every last one of their faces was just as dead white as that stone.

I went back home in no fit state, walked in the front door, and the phone started ringing. It was Jake. Judy'd called him from that mall to say she couldn't get Jimmy to get off his game machine and take her home. Jake asked to talk to Jimmy, but she said Jimmy wouldn't talk to anyone. Well, Jake came right on out once his shift ended—that was about two hours after the call—but he didn't find either one of them. Jimmy's car was still there in the parking lot, but no sign of Jimmy or Judy. That is, he thought he saw Jimmy once, but he was wrong about that, and he never saw Judy at all. He called Jimmy's friends' parents, the ones he knew about. None of them knew anything, except that one of them said his son, Jimmy's friend Chris, was out too late too, but what could you expect of kids these days? Judy—well, he wasn't sure who to call there; seems she'd been quarreling with the girls that used to be her friends, and with her father too, on account of her not having the kind of money they did to spend at that mall. Still, he tried a couple of places, and it did no good. There too he got told: "Kids these days…" He figured he was making a mountain out of a mole-hill, but he wanted to tell me he was worried.

I went to his house and kind of patted him on the back a little, and then I went to the mall. I swear it wasn't so far from the curb to the front door as it had been when I'd gone before.

I didn't see Jimmy in the line outside the booth. I cut the line, said I had to speak to my nephew about a family emergency. Some people muttered about calling the mall security, but then I guess they got a better look at my face and they let me get ahead of them and look inside the booth. And there was Jimmy, wearing a helmet that was plugged into the machine, still shooting at imaginary enemies. I knew him by the skinny height of him and the way he stood a little offsides, and by the scar on his elbow. When I shook his arm he ignored me. I kept shaking till he took the helmet off and looked at me. But it wasn't Jimmy's face that looked at me, just a blank kind of face with dead-white skin and cold skim-milk-blue eyes. That thing looked right through me and then put its helmet back on and went back to playing. It still had Jimmy's scar on its elbow, and Jimmy's beat-up red sneakers on its feet.

I looked and looked for Judy. I went through every store twice and then I hung around the girls' department in that blasted clothes store that Jake can't afford to buy from. I got some funny looks from girls that weren't Judy. They must have thought I was a nasty old man. Toward the back I saw a mannequin that caught my eye. It had a dead white face on it that couldn't ever have been anyone's, but it kind of stood up on its toes the way Judy used to, and its right arm was longer than its left like Judy's was, and there were calluses on its fingers right where Judy had hers from playing the violin.

Now, did you ever once in your life see a mannequin with calluses?

I knew it was her. I told myself I ought to steal her, but I'll tell you the honest truth, I couldn't make myself touch her. And I couldn't even bring the boy back, even if he really was Jimmy; one, he could probably knock me down, and two, if he couldn't, he could still yell and get me arrested for kidnapping or some such.

I drove over to Jake's place and told him what I'd seen, and he told me I was right off my head and added some things I won't repeat. I couldn't be sure he was wrong, but I couldn't be sure he was right either, and I figured I'd better get out of there before either of us said or did anything we couldn't take back.

"America the Beautiful" was on the radio as I turned off Jake's street, and as I listened I just came all over gooseflesh when they got to that one verse: "O beautiful for patriot dream that sees beyond the years thine alabaster cities gleam undimmed by human tears..."

I know what alabaster looks like–dead white–and I know the only way you can have no crying is to have no real people left.

I spent the next hour or so driving around town. I've lived here, boy and man, all of sixty-eight years, and I remember how things used to be. But they'd changed around me so slowly I hadn't seen them right.

Of course there were fewer fields and more stores and more little runaround roads with big houses on them than there used to be. I'd known that and grieved it, and I'd told myself I was just a sentimental old stick-in-the-mud. But I hadn't really noticed how many of the new buildings were white. The big new houses on the tiny lots, sure, but also some of the apartment buildings that folks like Ed and me had moved into after we lost their own places.

Yes, we'd both done some losing. Ed had lost more than I did, but then, he had more to lose: Mary Agnes chose him not me, and anyway he had the farm to start with. All my working and saving finally got me a house of my own, with a mortgage, when I was near on fifty. Then there was the crash and I was renting an apartment again, but how much did that matter for an old bachelor? I got a plot in the community garden so I could still grow some of my own truck, and whenever I could I got away into the woods, into the state land, to hunt and fish and traipse and feel like my own man. Ed came with me, sometimes.

I'd thought I was doing all right. But at the end of my little driving tour I came back to the apartment I was renting and I looked at the new coat of white paint they'd put on, and it seemed to me like it was glowing a little in the dark. So I figured I might be losing my mind after all, or else whatever was wrong was spreading so fast I couldn't do anything about it, and either way I didn't care to think about it.

I went up the stairs and let myself in and turned the TV on just to take my mind off things. The first channel I was on had an ad that reminded me too much of the Judy mannequin, so I changed the channel to a movie, something fast and exciting, I guess, if you like that sort of thing. I turned it up pretty loud, too, trying to drown out the nasty little voices in my mind. Like I said, I don't have hallucinations, but my brain chatters at me plenty, and that night I didn't like what it was saying. But my neighbor downstairs got to banging on the ceiling, and I realized it was kind of late for how much noise I was making.

I got up to turn the TV down—I don't know what happened to the remote control, it's been missing for months, or years maybe—and as I got up close to the screen it seemed like my skin looked kind of a nasty greenish-white in the screen glow. Well, I didn't care for that at all. I told myself if I just backed away and kept my eyes on the screen I wouldn't notice. Then I thought again about Jimmy in the game booth, about his pale skin and his face that was hardly a real face at all. I turned the TV off and snapped the light on, and I had a good look at myself in the bathroom mirror. I didn't much like what I saw. The features were my own, all right, but the eyes looked kind of glassy, and the skin way, way too pale.

That was last night. I didn't go to sleep—I didn't dare to. I spent the rest of the dark hours stuffing my car with everything I thought I'd want, and I packed up my big frame backpack with everything I thought I'd really need if anything happened to the car. Soon as it started to get light I called Jake. He hadn't heard from Jimmy or Judy. He'd called the police about them a few hours before, but I didn't think that would do him much good. I didn't say so. And then, as the light came up, I wrote this up. I'm going to run off a bunch of copies on my computer printer before I leave the computer behind for good, same as the apartment and the TV—they're all whiter than I like. I'll stuff envelopes in the mail to everyone I think might listen. I'll keep a few more—I figure on sticking them up in all the places I can think of that aren't creepy-white and that people can go into without having to spend money.

No, I'm not sure that the alabaster thing's about money. I'm not sure about much, except that I'm not going into any of the alabaster buildings again. I don't want to end up like Judy and Jimmy.

I don't much want to end up like Ed, either, if I'm right about what happened to him. Maybe people can get trapped by what they hate as much as by what they want. I don't know just what to do about that. If I figure it out, I'll tell you.

Oh yes, I'll be around. A lot of you have been good neighbors, and the rest of you still don't deserve to get eaten by the alabaster, and I may have been a bachelor all my life but I wasn't rightly cut out to be a hermit. You'll be seeing me at the library, and at the community garden, and at the Amish farm stands down south of town, and maybe at Rosie's little store so long as it stays Rosie's and a safe dark green, and if you head on over to the state forest you might see me there too. My tent's just big enough for one, but if you want help learning to hunt or fish or gather I can show you a thing or two.

That's if I make it out of here all right. There's one more thing I suppose I have to do, the way we've got the world set up now, after I put these warnings out but before I head for the woods. I've got to get the rest of my money out of that bank. I can't say I'm too easy in my mind about that. So if you get this letter, but you can't find me anywhere, I think you'd be smartest to stay right out of that bank for good and all. Leave whatever you've got in there, if you're lucky or unlucky enough to have anything in there at all, and start over again. Find some other way to make do for yourself and your neighbors. If enough of us did that, I guess we could maybe stop the alabaster, even if it took a lot of tears along the way.

PEAVEMAN'S LAMENT

JOANNA KOCH

I t was all because of the snack machine.
For two weeks, the shared vending machine in Peaveman's office building had been progressively and hopelessly
depleted. Chocolate bars gave way to nougat. Nougat surren-
dered to nuts. Nuts (unsalted) segued into expired cookies.
Cookies gave up the final ghost to sugar-free breath mints
and diet grape soda. Bereft, with no reasonable break time
options, Mark Anthony Peaveman decided to act.

Peaveman squeezed inside the niche that housed the
machine. There wasn't much room, but he was a slender guy
despite his eating habits. His lithe frame gained enough trac-
tion to push. Tile screeched. The top of the machine tilted.
The electrical cord snapped out of the socket like a whip.
Bottom heavy with two weeks of coins, the snack machine
rocked, making progress. Peaveman heaved it back and forth,
lumbering it out of the alcove and to the stairwell at the East
entrance. Slithering change inside the safe exaggerated the
shifting weight. A can of diet grape soda broke and spat
behind shatterproof glass.

The railing around the stairwell was an obstacle.

Peaveman bartered the uneven weight of the overloaded machine like a lever and see-sawed it over the metal bar. Down through the hollow core of the stairwell the snack machine plummeted for eleven full flights with a soft howl of displaced air. Peaveman found it strangely lovely, like a suicidal robot taking the final plunge to its digital demise. It hit the bottom and exploded like a missile blast.

"You're my hero."

Sweaty and wild-eyed, Peaveman turned towards the voice. It was one of the new hires, one of the cookie-cutter people who came and went so frequently at the job. Looks didn't matter at the call center, an aid to Peaveman's relative success. The kid admiring him had about five piercings in their face and twice as many colors in their hair. Peaveman disdained unconventional appearances that garnered attention. He was a firm believer in flying beneath the radar. These people seemed to be everywhere lately, he thought, like some peacock army amassing to combat tasteful tones and unmarred skin. He never knew which ones were boys and which ones were girls. He didn't understand why they made it so hard for people to figure out. He was at the point in his life where he wanted all of them, everyone, peacock or not, to leave him alone.

"Come on," the kid said. "You better book."

Shouts and footfalls flooded the stairwell. Peaveman agreed with the tug on his sleeve and followed the kid up three flights to an exit. The sign on the door read "Rooftop-- Restricted Area--Do Not Enter." Peaveman had never tried the door. In all his years at the job, he'd often wished to, imagining the dizzying liberation of the view high above the grind of everyday life. But the doorway was restricted. He'd always assumed it was locked.

The kid flew through with the grace of a hawk.

Peaveman limped up, aided by the bannister. He'd bruised

his knee battling with the snack machine, and he wasn't very limber after ages cramped in a cubicle. A few steps above, the kid's walk worried him into awkward pauses during his ascent. Their irregular, snaking gait seemed cleverly designed to trap Peaveman's nose between butt-cheeks. The unavoidable fragrance coming from the kid wasn't the usual eau de rotten patchouli that Peaveman associated with people of their type. It was more enigmatic. Alluring. Peaveman cringed with urgency. He needed to sort out if this person was under-aged, and some sort of tough girl or effeminate boy.

"You hulked out back there," the kid grinned at the top. They reached down to help Peaveman manage the last painful step. "Was it super awesome?"

Clouds would have been nice. The sun on the roof was blinding. Peaveman refused the lift and squinted at the kid. "I don't know."

"It looked so awesome. Did it feel like, you know, *Raawr!*" The kid made a weak giggling sound after the animal imitation and shook two slender fists in the air. The nails were not short. Not painted. The giggle was like a fresh jet of water.

The kid's magnetic joy splashed on Peaveman. He swallowed his lukewarm saliva, unsure if his attraction called his masculinity into question. His throat hitched as if he was ready to cry. Instead of giving in to the sudden desire to throw his arms around the kid and bury his face in every cleft, he stood up straight like a good soldier and said, "There was no other way. It had to be done."

The existence of the snack machine made Peaveman depressed under normal circumstances. Witnessing the contents dwindle and then remain irrevocably depleted with no hope of re-supply was too much pain to bear. Not only was the fake food bereft of nutrition and void of any flavor, but the mass-marketed chemical-additive-laced products designed to perpetuate an addictive, momentary gratification were almost all gone. The loss of what was barely adequate to begin with was intolerable.

Peaveman said, "I had to take a stand. Guess I lost my job."

"Don't worry about that. They'll never know it's you."

Reassurance that he would not escape employment was worse than the thought of being fired. Peaveman protested. "They'll know. They'll see that I never came back from my break."

"Half the people hired don't come back from their breaks. Like, you know, ever." The kid giggled again and Peaveman censored the wish to dive at them and wrestle the kid into torrents of erotic laughter, rolling around on the rooftop, ignoring the rocks, broken glass, and bird shit. If only he could see the kid better he'd feel less upset by his impulses.

"I always come back. They'll know."

Peaveman wasn't sure if he spoke from fatalism or hope. He pictured write-ups in the news after his arrest. Some catchphrase akin to *going postal* might emerge as common slang, maybe *snack attack* or *candy crash* or *vendor avenger*. An outbreak of copycats destroying vending machines and snack bars and junk food dispensers all across the United States. Gumballs strewn across the highways, La Brea tar pits of dried soda trapping loud children inside schools and playgrounds, cereal aisles in grocery stores and quick marts doused in gasoline, storehouses of faux-nutrition going up in flames. Peaveman smiled at the thought.

"I'll cover for you," the kid said. "Be your alibi."

Peaveman tried to get a better look. Sunlight glinted off the many piercings. The glare made it impossible to gaze straight into the kid's face. If Peaveman stared too long, he saw a ring of fire encircling their head.

"How old are you? You didn't tell me your name."

"Hey, listen, I'll say I got sick and you gave me a lift home. They can't argue with helping me out. You have a car, right?"

"Not anymore. Wife took all that. I take the bus now." Peaveman rested his eyes and scanned the miniature streets twelve stories below. They crawled with toy cars and scurrying ant-people who carried tiny pheromone-laden briefcases that marked the trail towards success. He leaned over the ledge a little too far. "I think I hear sirens."

The kid leaned with him. "They won't search up here. You're safe with me."

"Until tomorrow or the next day. Then what?" Peaveman leaned further into the breeze and let the wind wrap his aching head in the kid's peculiarly soothing scent. Maybe masculinity didn't matter anymore. Maybe nothing did. Peaveman smiled at the kid tentatively and then dropped his eyes down to the street.

The ant farm activity had increased. Peaveman was glad to be above it for once. On the rooftop, he was outside of the glass looking in. The colorful creature next to him shimmered within reach. Without looking up again, he said: "At least jail will be a change. I almost wish I'd done something worse."

The air shifted. The scent withdrew. Peaveman turned to make sure the kid was still there. The sirens below halted with a blip. Emergency flashers went out like dying fireflies in contrast to the kid's overwhelming brilliance. Peaveman tried to look. The kid blasted his eyes like the glare from a furnace.

They knelt and bowed. "Walk upon my sword."

Peaveman didn't see a sword, but he heard it. A chorus of light singing. Bright air whistling in his ears.

"Why me?"

The kid's clear voice rolled across the rooftop like a cool wind. "I won't let them take you from me."

"Shit, I need a girlfriend, not a guardian angel." Peaveman shielded his eyes and tried to glimpse the kid, holding his hands like a visor. "What are you supposed to be?"

"Nothing," the kid said. "No one."

Peaveman's throat went dry and tight. "I need to go."

He turned. Tears smudged the corners of his eyes. He almost collided with a person standing right behind him. He edged sideways after the jolt. He didn't realize anyone else was up here. His elbow made contact with a fleshy midriff and his foot bumped a shoe on his other side. Peaveman recoiled. He was boxed in. People were everywhere. They lurked between the carbines and rooftop vents. They huddled under the shallow awnings of equipment casings. They stood in piles of debris and pigeon dung, crowded in a dumb mass under the sun. They faced Peaveman in silence.

As if he were a monster cornered by an accusing mob, Peaveman braced to make his villain's proclamation. *Here I am, you cowards, you sheep. You found me. You'll thank me when you wake up out of your stupor! There's nothing! Nothing!*

His voice caught when he noticed the blood spattered on their clothes. The snack machine must have flung shrapnel on impact and caused an outrageous number of injuries. Stuttering with guilt, Peaveman tried to apologize to a young woman nearby. Her arm dangled in a very wrong manner. He couldn't get the words out. Below the bicep, her flesh was abraded and skinless. He thought he saw a sliver of bone. Peaveman cried out in disgust and remorse.

He cowered. The mob surrounded him. Not one person remained unharmed.

Peaveman's eyes flew in every direction seeking escape. Everywhere he looked, dislocated shoulders, shattered knees. Splintered skulls leaking chunky, liquefied contents, erupting from half a face. Between the wounded who stood upright, Peaveman glimpsed dismembered suggestions of prone victims. Too twisted to stand, their limbs floundered like bad acrobats. Some were little more than crimson puddles of hands, hair, and meat. Peaveman swung around and shrank from the throng.

"No, I'm sorry, I can't—it wasn't me." Peaveman found his voice. But he had no defense. He was the coward. He was the sheep. He put his face in his hands, closed his eyes, and wept.

It couldn't be true. He'd seen the snack machine fall. The empty stairwell was clear before it dropped. The doors on each floor had automatic closures according to fire safety regulations. They swung in toward the stairwell. He didn't understand how they'd blast open from the snack machine's impact.

He cried into his guilty hands. "What do you want from me?"

The throng didn't answer.

Peaveman raised his remorseful face. One exploding snack machine had crushed and mangled this vast mob ready to swarm him.

But they didn't swarm. They hovered, close yet indifferent.

Like all the people in Peaveman's life.

He was used to it. He was sick of it. He was sick of being used to it.

He screamed. His voice cracked. "Okay, I did it. Come and get me you assholes. Do your worst!"

Nothing happened.

Peaveman shoved. The bodies swayed like heavy carcasses and came back to rest. They formed an impenetrable wall of human meat. Pressed against the ledge, Peaveman begged the kneeling kid for help.

"Get them away from me. Get me out of here. What's happening?"

"Come forward," the kid said. "And tread upon my

sword." No longer invisible, the sword stretched across the gravel rooftop floor. Peaveman heard it singing, saw it glimmering.

The kid was now unbearable to behold, made of light, silver, steel, and jewels. Peaveman suspected a siren sent to lure him to doom; yet the sword sang his name with singular knowledge. The indifferent mob that crowded him off the rooftop was no different than the crowds that railroaded him out of his life and out of his love and into doom as he'd known it too often. Through the disappointment of others, through guilt, through loss, through litigation, the kid's image burned brighter than a star. Peaveman defied his anonymous annihilation and grabbed the hilt of an intimate damnation he hoped to call his very own.

He stepped onto the sword. Pain shot through his body. The blade swung over the ledge. Peaveman balanced in midair. He gasped in fear. The kid blinded him with fire. Now molten inside, his agony turned into bliss. It slid through him and out of him, soaking the sword. In one gesture, the kid lifted the sword, cleaved Peaveman in half and clad him in gold. They both fell.

As the sword sliced through the air, the kid stripped. Peaveman knew them and needed them without indifference or sorrow. The kid bucked and clawed. With the many arms of a spider, the kid spun Peaveman into a sarcophagus that held the undisclosed riches of a feral identity. Concentrated inside his casing, Peaveman liquefied and supplied hot magma to his host.

Falling was not flying. The sidewalk grit of the commercial district rushed at Peaveman's skull. Encased in gold as the city herself was encased in concrete, Peaveman acknowledged the consequences of falling. "What will happen when we meet again?"

The voice of the kid answered with a tittering giggle

afterward. "Then you will know us, and through us, you will also be revealed."

The fall was fast. Stillness held the center. Heavier by the second, gold and glitter glorified Peaveman's pulse. Liquid in rushing air, no way out, no chance to flee, to plead for life, falling, falling without reprieve, falling. Peaveman froze.

The molten gold inside Peaveman hardened into brittle mesh. The kid gripped him with all their arms before the bones collapsed. They clenched the tense sensation of Peaveman's petrified organs. The kid pulled out the soft parts and left a quivering shell like a water balloon. Peaveman's panic burst upon impact. The kid savored this part, drank it in like an endless diet grape soda and crushed the empty can when it was drained.

Peaveman met the ground upside down in a decapitating crunch.

In the moment between brain death and the crack of his neck, before Peaveman's aural imprint joined the kid's collection in the skyscraper's hungry rooftop maw, after Peaveman's cervical vertebrae ripped apart and his carotid arteries popped; in that brief pause when Peaveman's body stopped and his severed head bounded with autonomous joy on a trajectory of total freedom; for that instant, Peaveman lamented that his richest intimacy had been in falling, and that as his head hit the street for the third time, he knew the gold hidden within him would shatter and forever be lost.

CORPOS!

M. LOPES DA SILVA

W e live in its bones now and think ourselves safe
enough, believing that no necromancer could come
and resurrect this monster, but that's why this story must be
told. This is resurrection season. The wind prickles with it.
New generations must be taught to spurn concrete idols.
How to blunt the rebar with mallets when it sprouts up
through the earth after a dry spell. How to pour water down
the worming bases to rust them to the roots.

Regret is an unrusted thing. It glints.

Now is the perfect time to feel regret; there is no better
one! So we ask ourselves, again and again and again: why did
we create such a horrible thing? Why? Because we thought
we would be safe. Beyond safe, we thought we would be
comforted and loved by these looming giants. We wanted to
be small always, like children, protected by the guardians we
built. And we needed the work, the employers said, or we
would be godless, or worse, useless. We needed the jobs, we
were told. So we did them.

We poured the concrete. We placed the rebar. We
soldered the wires and installed the windows. We didn't

know then that every glass square we fitted was another scale, glistening and thick along its concrete hide. But even if we had known, who among us would have forfeited their paycheck to say something? We built its vascular system, and told ourselves that it was only plumbing. We built its lungs, and said we'd paneled meeting rooms. Then we gave it teeth. We had no excuse for the teeth. They were *teeth*.

To our great shame, we made Corpos. We cannot be allowed to forget that.

When the building was done, and the higher ups called for a sacrifice to launch this project—one necessary to get things up and running, otherwise they wouldn't be able to afford to pay our bonuses. We were uncomfortable, but invested. We'd spent all that time. Months and years and lifetimes. All that energy and hard work. And we needed the bonuses; things were always tight for us in a way that the employers never seemed to be able to understand. It was reasonable, we decided, to make a small sacrifice. After all, we had sacrificed so much already, one more couldn't hurt.

We thought maybe we would draw lots or take part in some kind of lottery, but they had a method. They called it an Evaluation. They fussed around and lined us up this way and that while Accounting tallied up our relative expendability. It was a humiliating experience. Our employers decided who among us they could afford to lose. We were priced like meat, counted like money. They announced over hidden speakers how much we were worth as we congregated in front of the slumbering structure, and the most shameful part is that I was, for a moment, *proud* when they told me my relative value to the company.

Now, I know. Now I understand that you should never be proud of what people think they can take from you. Back then I was so hungry all the time: for food, for love, for approval. We were all kept that way. The employers liked us that way, too—they said it made us ambitious. Our parents were just like them. At night they would tell us what the employers had told them, and we would huddle around their ideas as if they could keep us warm while we shivered by our broken thermostats. We praised the concrete idols passed down from the higher-ups and whispered our wishes to them before bed.

We wanted so much!

We cannot forget that so many of us stood there and nervously let ourselves be appraised and sorted. A few among us fought, but there should have been more, and these few brave souls were quickly dragged away from the lines by security.

What I am saying is *I* should have fought. I should have done everything in my power to fight this. We should have become chaos. We should have done anything but what we did.

Through the glass we could see the lobby, sleek marble with a carpet the color of arteries. I still see it in my dreams at night. The dreams don't leave me. I don't think they ever will.

———

IT WAS HAPPENING SO QUICKLY—TOO quickly! There was a T-shirt cannon. They'd made it all a game. A catered event. Popular music pumped like a pulse in between the names and numbers. Hot dogs were everywhere, so many that torn shreds of blistered sausage were pulped underfoot. We still wanted to get our bonuses. We weren't sure when we were going to get them or how much they would exactly be, but we were hopeful. A T-shirt with "CORPOS" and a simple outline of the thing we'd built printed on it hit me in the side of the head.

They picked thirteen employees for the first group. There was a raffle for a golf cart that somebody won, and a man was screaming in excitement when they herded the thirteen into the elevator. I was fumbling for my T-shirt between my feet. Then the doors shut and nobody could see what was going on.

It wasn't clear what had happened at first—not explicitly clear. A woman standing next to me said: "Maybe they'll be working at the top now. We don't know! They always look out for us." Then the ground began to rumble, bucking the soles of our feet. We fell into each other or scraped dirt. The music was still joyful, but we were discordant.

"Earthquake!" someone shouted. But it wasn't. We looked up and saw the thing we'd built come to life.

Pylons and concrete tore free from their foundations, leaving raw tangles of rebar and wire dangling. Glass shattered, sending shards down among us. One shard nearly entered a man's skull, only to shear off his ear and embed deeply inside his chest. Another shard went through a woman's neck. There was blood everywhere. We slid in it as we tried to escape.

A deep, terrible scream tore the world apart. Not our human screams, but an inhuman one. I covered my ears, but couldn't escape the horrible sound. The scream was an advertisement, piercing our brains with its hideous jingle. The looming, distorted human skull at the end of a serpentine tangle of steel and glass angled its lit windows to peer down at us, then parted its teeth (slick with exactly *what* we were too far away to say) and roared once more.

———

THE BONUSES they gave us were so small that they barely made a dent in the debt that all of our sudden, urgent health

care demanded. None of us escaped without injury, and
hardly any of us could afford to properly treat our injuries.
We got worse. Everyone knew someone who came down
with infections they couldn't afford to treat and died. Their
families couldn't even afford to hold funerals for them.

But Corpos was in motion! The giant abomination
roamed through our neighborhoods at all hours, making the
earth tremble in its wake. I spent most nights awake,
listening to Corpos as it made its way through the streets,
shivering as the quaking grew closer. My heartbeat in every
cell of my body when Corpos paused by my apartment, and
my lone room flooded with the fluorescent glow of the giant
construction's searching lights. The fear. Then learning how
to move again once Corpos had moved on, the stiffness in
my joints incredible. My body a tangle of pain. Every night
like this!

The part most people don't believe is this: we kept going
to work.

With our fresh debts and agonies, we needed the money
more than ever. We needed paychecks to get rid of the pain.
We needed jobs that didn't require us to build things
anymore, because our bodies couldn't take the long hours
and stress. We needed office jobs.

Every day we went to work and prayed that there would
be no more Evaluations. Those prayers went unanswered.
Corpos had to eat, we were told. The machine had to be fed.
We were too uneducated to know how an economy worked
in a capitalist society.

And we were *protected* by Corpos. We were so safe!
Weren't we grateful for our safety? Our paychecks? Everything the company *did* for us?

So every day we commuted to Corpos, and took the same
elevator that took the thirteen, and went to work. We tried
to focus on documents and spreadsheets while the office

lurched and pitched around us. We tried to ignore the fact that we worked inside the body of a monster, and that every task we performed made it stronger. Every line of data that we corrected served some arcane purpose. Scientists among us now speculate that we were a kind of digestive tract: human bacteria processing what Corpos fiscally ate and spat out again. And sometimes thirteen more of us were chosen by the higher-ups and ended up taking the elevator to a different floor, the floor with teeth, and those thirteen were added to our memorial walls and forlorn social media updates.

Our grief had nowhere to go. We were always grieving, always in pain, always hungry. We saw pictures on our phones of large homes with wood flooring and marble countertops, and our employers living in them. We looked at our own crumbling plaster rental boxes and laughed.

The thirteen were mythic: without bodies, they had no funerals. As months went by, and sacrifices for the company continued, memorials for the missing began to outnumber those for the confirmed dead.

———

THE END of Corpos did not begin with me. I am not the one who resisted first. It took me a while to become brave like the others.

We started meeting after work. Behind local closed businesses, in parking lots and alleys. We spoke to each other about what had happened to us, and our friends and family. And the more we shared, the more we realized how much we had lost.

We were angry. In mourning and in pain.

And then the morning came.

———

IT STARTED ON ANOTHER FLOOR—NOT mine. By the time the movement came to our floor we were clinging to our desks for dear life. Corpos moved roughly, far more violently than usual. Computer monitors tore free from their anchored positions on our desks, sending gouts of oily gore everywhere.

The stairwell entrance door burst open. A C.E.O. lurched out, panic bending his pale, damp brow.

"Hide me!" he demanded.

But there was another sound, muffled but persistent, swelling in volume just behind him. We clung to the furniture in a barnacle hush. We waited to hear what the new sound brought with it. We did not have to wait long.

The door banged open again. Office workers from the floor above us spilled out, their voices loud: "Send the C.E.O. up!"

One of the three elevator doors on our floor softly chimed and opened. The uncalled car had no passengers. It waited.

"Send the C.E.O. up!"

The C.E.O. tried to run, but the room went up, down, sideways and the people from the other floor were scrambling after him. Then we were, too. We abandoned our desks and stumbled across the office to reach him. His scream went raw and rasping once our hands descended. We held him firmly. The elevator waited for us. We weren't even near the button—the car held itself.

The sharp stink of piss came from him as we tossed him into the waiting car, and the door finally closed shut.

We cheered. The C.E.O.'s scream went fine and thin as he lifted away from us. But Corpos shook and screamed its jingle into the broad blue day, and we knew we had so much more to do.

So many floors. So many executives.

Floor by floor we descended. Pieces of Corpos fell everywhere, smashing up whole blocks of concrete and asphalt. Destroying our city. An apartment building collapsed beneath the weight of debris. Then more joined the first. The air was just broken buildings that wouldn't settle. It stayed like that for days.

When Corpos died, it took out everything it could demolish. Everything it could touch. The monster would not die alone.

When it fell, we let ourselves out of its corpse.

————

BUT IT IS NOT DEAD! Never make that mistake. We may live in its bones now, but bones belong to the living and the dead, and an idea cannot die.

Corpos can always be resurrected.

WRITER BIOS

Clark Boyd lives and works in the Netherlands. His fiction has appeared in High Shelf Press, Fatal Flaw Magazine, Scare Street, Havok, Frost Zone Zine, and various DBND and Jazz House horror anthologies. One of his short stories has also been chosen for inclusion in this year's Bouchercon mystery and crime anthology. Before turning to fiction, he spent two decades writing, editing, reporting, and producing international news stories for US public radio and the BBC World Service. You can find him at www.clark-boyd.com.

Hailey Piper is the author of horror novel *Queen of Teeth*, her short story collection *Unfortunate Elements of My Anatomy*, and horror novellas *The Worm and His Kings, Benny Rose, the Cannibal King,* and *The Possession of Natalie Glasgow*. She is a member of the HWA with short fiction in *Year's Best Hardcore Horror*, Dark Matter Magazine, The Arcanist, and elsewhere. She lives with her wife in Maryland. Find her at www.haileypiper.com or on Twitter via @HaileyPiperSays.

Corey Farrenkopf lives on Cape Cod with his wife, Gabrielle, and works as a librarian. He is the fiction editor for the Cape Cod Poetry Review. His fiction has been published in Tiny Nightmares, The Southwest Review, Wigleaf, Flash Fiction Online, Bourbon Penn, *Campfire Macabre,* and elsewhere. To learn more, follow him on twitter @CoreyFarrenkopf or on the web at CoreyFarrenkopf.com.

Nathaniel Lee lives in Oregon with his family and too many board games. He puts words into various orders, and sometimes people give him money afterward. No one knows why. You can follow his website for free fiction and updates at www.mirrorshards.net.

Ilene Goldman lives in northern Illinois, where she is closely supervised by her canine editorial assistants. You can find her on Twitter @ilenegold and on the web at www.ilene-goldman.com.

Tim Kane loves things that creep and crawl. His first published book is non-fiction, *The Changing Vampire of Film and Television*, tracing the history of vampires in television and movies. Most recently published stories appear in Exchange Students, Lovecraftia and Attack of the Killer... Find out more at www.timkanebooks.com.

Brennan LaFaro is a horror reader/writer living in south eastern Massachusetts with his wife, two sons, and his hounds. An avid lifelong reader and book reviewer, Brennan also co-hosts the Dead Headspace podcast. His debut novella, *Slattery Falls* is set to be released in Summer 2021 through Silver Shamrock Publishing. You can find him on twitter at @brennanlafaro.

Derek Des Anges is an emerging cross-genre author and occasional journalist from London. He studied Creative and Media Writing at Middlesex University and has spent most of the intervening years diligently forgetting everything he learnt. His work has now appeared in a diverse range of publications, including Vulture Bones Magazine, Calyx's And Lately, The Sun, and Feral Cat Publishers' Dear Leader Tales.

Laurel Hightower grew up in Kentucky, attending college in California and Tennessee before returning home to horse country, where she lives with her husband, son, and a rescue pitbull. She works as a paralegal in a mid-size firm, wrangling litigators by day and writing at night. A bourbon and beer girl, she's a fan of horror movies and true life ghost stories. She is the author of *Whispers in the Dark* and *Crossroads*, co-edited the charity anthology *We Are Wolves,* and her short fiction has appeared in several anthologies.

Donald McCarthy is a writer from New York. His work has happened in magazines, newspapers, and books. A complete look at his publications can be found at http://www. donaldmccarthy.com.

Ty Zink is a trans anarchist storyteller. On occasion, he'll write those stories down. Zink's writing leans to urban fantasy and magic realism, influenced by his usual medium of tabletop roleplaying games. He's involved in collective organizing and education in his Midwestern hometown, where he lives with his husband and cats. Zink can be found on Twitter at @LizardBarbarian.

Dustin Walker has worked as a dishwasher, a news reporter and a tech marketer. But he's most passionate about writing gritty crime and horror stories. Dustin's fiction has appeared in Yellow Mama, Dark Moon Digest, Pulp Modern and on The NoSleep Podcast. He lives on Vancouver Island, Canada, with his wife and daughter.

Noah Lemelson is a young speculative fiction writer working out of Los Angeles. Noah received his MFA in Creative Writing from the California Institute of the Arts in May 2019, where he studied under the mentorship of Brian

Evenson. His debut steampunk fantasy novel, The Sightless City, is set to be released July 20th 2021 from Tiny Fox Press.

Tom Nicholson is an ESL teacher originally from the UK and currently living in Ho Chi Minh City, Vietnam. His work has previously been shortlisted for the IT Tallaght Short Story Prize and has featured in several journals, including publications from Scarlet Leaf Review, Pavor Press, and more. Tom is currently working on his first full length novel and spends most of his spare time worrying about the editing process.

The infantile left -wing adventurist **David Stevens** is a spectre haunting Sydney, Australia, where he foments revolution with his wife and those of his children who have not yet thrown off their yokes and broken their chains. His earnest treatises of devastating analysis have appeared amongst other places in Vastarien, Crossed Genres, Aurealis, Three-Lobed Burning Eye, Pseudopod, Andromeda Spaceways Magazine, Cafe Irreal, and several anthologies. It is historically inevitable that you will visit his ~~blog~~ manifesto at davidstevens.info.

Tiffany Michelle Brown is a California-based writer who once had a conversation with a ghost over a pumpkin beer. Her fiction has been featured by Sliced Up Press, Cemetery Gates Media, Fright Girl Summer, and the NoSleep Podcast. She is the author of "Easy as Pie," a self-published short story that explores love, death, and the consequences of holding too tightly to earthly memories. Tiffany lives near the beach with her husband, Bryan, their pups, Biscuit and Zen, and their combined collections of books, board games, and general geekery. Follow her adventures at tiffanymichellebrown.wordpress.com.

Joanna Michal Hoyt lives on a Catholic Worker farm in northern New York State that tries to live an alternative to the consumer culture and practice neighborliness. She spends her days tending goats, gardens, and guests, and her evenings reading and writing odd stories. Her short speculative fiction has appeared in publications including Mysterion, On Spec, and Daily Science Fiction. Some of those stories can be read free through the links at https://joannamichalhoyt.com/. Her novel *Cracked Reflections*, set amongst immigrant millhands in Massachusetts during the textile strikes of 1912, will be published by Propertius Press in May 2021.

Joanna Koch writes literary horror and surrealist trash. Shirley Jackson Award finalist, author of *The Wingspan of Severed Hands* and *The Couvade*, their short fiction appears in *Year's Best Hardcore Horror 5*, *Not All Monsters*, and many others. Find Joanna at horrorsong.blog and on Twitter @horrorsong.

M. Lopes da Silva is a bisexual poet, author, and artist from Los Angeles. She's messy and likes to make the written equivalent of mud pies with folk tales and queer camp and splatterpunk all smashed up together. Her fiction has appeared in Electric Literature, *Glass and Gardens: Solarpunk Summers*, and *Nightscript Vol. IV* and *V*. Unnerving recently published her novella *Hooker:* a pro-queer, pro-sex work, feminist retrowave pulp thriller about a bisexual sex worker hunting a serial killer in 1980s Los Angeles using hooks as her weapons of choice.

EDITOR BIOS

Ian A. Bain (he/him) is a writer of dark fiction living in Muskoka, Ontario. Ian enjoys Horror, coffee, and long walks through the swamp with his wife and undead dog. Ian's writing has appeared in various anthologies, magazines, and podcasts. Ian can be stalked online at @bainwrites on Twitter.

Anthony Engebretson is a speculative fiction writer and avid raccoon lover from Nebraska. His work has been published in several anthologies including *Spring into SciFi* (2018 and 2019) and *The Rabbit Hole: Weird Stories Vol. 1*. You can find him on twitter @AnthonyJEngebr1 or his blog: raccoonalleyblog.wordpress.com

J.R. Handfield (@jrhandfield on Twitter) lives in Central Massachusetts with his wife, his son, and his cat; not necessarily in that order. His work can be found in *Hundred Word Horror: Home* and *Hundred Word Horror: Beneath*, both from Ghost Orchid Press, with hopefully more to come.

Eric Raglin (he/him) is a speculative fiction writer, podcaster for Cursed Morsels, and horror educator from Nebraska. He frequently writes about queer issues, the terrors of capitalism, and body horror. His work has been published in Novel Noctule, Dread Stone Press, and Shiver. His debut short story collection *Nightmare Yearnings* is out

September 2021. Find him at ericraglin.com or on Twitter @ericraglin1992.

Marcus Woodman (he/him) is a writer, illustrator, and historian from Nebraska. His work spans genres, but all touch on a queer experience, and his debut story was published in the *Trans-Galactic Bike Ride* anthology. He lives with his husband and their two cats, and writes to the jeers of blue jays outside. More of his work can be found at jackdawmarc.wordpress.com, and he can be found at Twitter @jackdawmarc.

CPSIA information can be obtained
at www.ICGtesting.com
Printed in the USA
BVHW080045070521
606650BV00003B/354